NEXT DOOR

a collection of twelve twisted tales and one true story

KIMBERLY DAVIS BASSO

PRAISE FOR BIRTH AND OTHER SURPRISES

"The best incentive for birth control a teenager will ever get."

— JUNE BOWER-BARRET, AUTHOR OF
WHEN THE VOICES IN MY HEAD
FORMED A SUPPORT GROUP

"Honest, no holds barred account of child bearing. I laughed so hard I cried."

— ERIN MATTINGLY, DOULA SERVICES

"Basso makes you laugh out loud and hard... only after that you realize through her humor she brings you into the greater truth, that is Basso's gift."

— WILLIAM QUIGLEY, AUTHOR OF JOY
BLISS THIS

*for Sandra
and the spiders dancing on her dress*

THE KING OF CAPE COD

JIMMY COULDN'T KEEP UP, THERE WAS NO WAY. HIS brothers disappeared down the beach before he got off the boardwalk. Figures. He kicked at a clump of sea grass and walked in the other direction, away from the crowd. Not easy to do in August on the Cape, but there were enough dunes and lumps of sand to hide in. Let them worry, let them think about what they'd done. He wasn't sure he could stay away until lunch time, which was what it would take in order to make them truly scared. Even then he couldn't be sure they'd notice until they were back at the cottage waiting for PB&J's and salty chips on the picnic table out back.

He stopped altogether. No point in rushing. His feet were burning from the walk two blocks away; he should have known he couldn't go without sandals like his brothers. "Wimp!" they yelled when he had to stop every ten feet to find a shadow or sit on his butt and lift his feet in the air to cool them.

"Stupid, come on!" He heard Scotty holler from the edge of the water, where they were pushing the Sunfish into the waves. He looked behind him.

"Yeah, you stupid. Let's go dumb ass."

He ran over the sand, ignoring his burnt feet and splashed into the water, then came up short, unsure of what he was supposed to do. The Sunfish was his brother's pride and joy, and even though it looked like a child's drawing of a sailboat, just a plastic base about ten feet long with a single sail, Jimmy still stood there waiting for instruction.

"Push, stupid."

His three brothers piled on and started to unroll the small sail while he shoved from the back. Then he stopped and let his feet dig into the soft sand. Gripping the rimmed edge of the boat, he leaned as far and as hard as he could backwards toward the shore. The water was at his chest, and the boat bobbled, but he forced it to pause.

"Can I come?" he asked, fingers white-knuckled on the wet, slippery edge, "Can I come sail with you?"

Three heads snapped around.

"Can I...?" he swallowed and waited. All three hopped off the boat into the water, waist deep for them. They stared at him as he stopped it from moving. He added quickly, "I'm not big. You always tell me I'm not big."

"That's right little dick. You're not big at all."

"Think he's ready?"

"One way to find out."

"Wait, wait, what are you, wait –"

"Don't let go of that boat, little dick, don't you dare let go."

He held on with both hands as he felt his feet get kicked out from under him and his body sank into the water. They had the timing perfect; they brought his head up and when he collected himself enough to holler, they shoved him back beneath the surface, mouth still open, salt water pouring into his throat. Dunk, rise, gasp, dunk. They finally stopped for a moment so he could breathe and used that time to pile seaweed on top of his head. Eyes streaming, throat raw, Scotty held him up by the armpits. Wet sand mixed with the seaweed and made his head hard to lift. He could barely see past the curtain of green and brown drooping in front of his eyes.

"Gentlemen, I give you the King of Cape Cod."

"Nice crown, King."

"Shut up Tommy."

Scotty held the boat as the other two dragged Jimmy onto the sand and flung him toward the girl cousins, sitting in a circle rubbing baby oil on each other. The girls shrank away but didn't bother to shriek. The youngest is never a threat. By the time he rolled over and looked, the boat was already past the break, the tiny sail unrolled. The three boys were still laughing, mouths open wide, but they were too far away to hear over the waves. He'd show them. He'd find something really cool, cooler than Scotty found yesterday.

"Not cooler than this," he heard Scotty's voice in his head as he pictured him waving a whole but utterly dead crab. Yeah, that would be hard to beat. An entire dead crab was a tough one, particularly since it was covered in ants and had the added bonus of showing up right near the girl cousins, who screamed and threw sand in their faces until they agreed to "GO AWAY!" He wandered up the beach and headed into the dunes. Anything left on the shore would be too picked over by the seagulls to matter much. He'd have to look inland, and that meant sand fleas. They chewed without mercy, tiny bites without end.

A seagull kept him company as he walked, trying to rub the grit out of his hair, cropped short for summer. Nothing much to see at first, an old T-shirt, and then a diaper, which he considered briefly but realized it too would likely end up on his head, so he left it.

He was grabbing small rocks and chucking them toward

the shore when he saw the bowl. Smooth and round, and too perfect to be a shell, which is what he imagined when he first saw it peeking from the dune. He pulled it out and tilted it to drain the sand. It was white and thick, and made of rock maybe? Something harder than plastic. It didn't matter, a bowl wasn't going to impress his brothers. He looked around anyway, just in case they were close enough to hear, but the dune was high enough that even the waves were muffled so there was no point shouting his discovery. Still, a bowl was something. He walked along, adding rocks to it, listening to them rattle and bounce. The seagull walked along behind him now, waiting for whatever it was in the bowl. He ran at her to shoo her away, his brothers told him all sea gulls were girls and that's why they were so screechy, but she just lifted off and landed a few feet out of reach. His treasures dumped out of the bowl when he lunged for her, so he started over again. A small brick red rock, no longer than his fingernail. The inside twist of a tiny whelk shell. It was hard to decide what to keep. Something too cool and it would be taken away. Something too dumb and it would be ignored. A fiddler crab claw next, and then a dead fiddler crab, and then a mass of living fiddler crabs swarming over something covered in brown seaweed. He squished the bulbs of the seaweed as he took a closer look, holding his breath against the stench. Something smooth stuck out of the pile, and he slid it out to check. Just a popsicle stick with a joke he already knew.

He placed the bowl next to him on the path out of the dune and waved his arms at the seagull to back off, still staring at the pile of seaweed. Maybe there was other stuff, maybe jewelry, or coins, or maybe someone had had a picnic or dropped a wallet or something and—it was peeking out of a mass of seaweed, and covered in hermit crabs, but was that another bit of white under all that wet brown? Probably just a cigarette butt, he told himself. He brushed at the crabs and they skittered away leaving a rough, white plate? Maybe? No, it was too curved, another bowl? He reached for it and felt something slimy bump past his wrist. Jellyfish he thought and snapped his hand to his chest as quick as he could. But it wasn't a jelly, in fact it almost looked like a sea cucumber, but the color was wrong, and it was way too far from the waves and the hard packed sand to be slimy. Cucumbers were usually right at the shoreline, left behind by the tide like limp dicks. He'd had enough of them thrown at his face to remember. His brothers called them jimmies of course, which he knew meant him but also meant something bad, something else bad, something to do with girls by the way they were laughing. He poked the slimy-but-not-a-sea-cucumber thing with a finger and the pointy end of it curled toward itself and gently grasped his fingertip.

He startled and said, "Hello."

He didn't expect an answer and he didn't get one.

He eased his hand away again, but it held on, stretching and stretching until he was sure it would snap. Fine. Using one hand, he cleared the seaweed away from where the thing stuck into it, and that's when he saw the rest of the bowl. It had eye sockets, and a jaw line and oh my god it was a skull an actual skull and suddenly the air became very still. The seagull rested a few feet away, small black eyes watching.

Nobody, nobody had ever found anything as cool as this, this blew the bowl away, this blew away his brother getting to second base with whatshername, this was better than... better than stolen cigarettes. A skull. An actual skull. It wasn't another bowl at all. He stood up to grab it and found the cucumber thing was still holding his finger. He looked closer, tiny suction cups. Gold mine. This dune was a gold mine. He had a skull, he had a tentacle, his heart was beating faster and his ego dreamed of their shocked faces. He dug at the seaweed pile for the end of the tentacle and found it, pulled it free. It hung off his finger and he flipped it back and forth as he grabbed the bowl with his left hand and brought it back toward the skull. It was a little tricky, he wasn't any good with his left hand, and he didn't want to hurt the tentacle, but he managed to prop the skull up on the pile and get it looking at him. It was a pretty good skull; it had all the top teeth and most of the jaw. Cool. Was that a bit of flesh, nope, just a bit of seaweed. He flipped the bowl against his side and placed it upside down on top of the skull. Perfect fit. Perfect fit! He had a whole skull! They were gonna be so jealous. He imagined holding the skull up over his head, his treasure, his mighty – his daydream was interrupted by the tentacle falling off his finger. He'd forgotten all about it. It was cool, no question, and he wasn't willing to leave it behind. Let them be amazed by the tentacle and then he'd blow them away with the skull. Too bad he didn't have a shirt on to hide it under.

Carefully, he picked the tentacle up again without touching the suckers. It was hefty, but thin, and although it was wet, the sand didn't stick. He knew just what to do. He carefully wrapped it around his head, tucking the ends in to form a crown. Now he was the king. Or least, the king of their rental cottage. Didn't matter, he was the king. He wiggled his head back and forth, and the tentacle stayed put. Wicked. They were gonna be so mad they left him behind. He picked up the skull, top and bottom, and held it like a chalice to his chest. The seagull approved and he bowed to her, until he remembered that he was the king.

As he stepped onto the path back to the water, he felt the tentacle wiggle down his forehead a bit, and he froze. Nope, all good, it wasn't going anywhere. He scampered back toward the beach, dreaming of the scene at home, everyone at the picnic table, his mom hollering, his brothers so jealous. Good. He felt so good, skull clasped tight, one hand over, one hand under, tentacle crowning his forehead. He was the King of Cape Cod. He puffed out his chest, and felt the tentacle tighten. And tighten again. And then it began to squeeze.

When the older boys returned for lunch, they waited for their brother, concerned over what was sure to be a tattle tale session.

When their mother asked where he was, they said they didn't know. When the girl cousins tattled on them, they said to shut up or they'd make them shut up. When their father asked where he was, they said, maybe he went for a swim?

When the police asked where he was, they said he walked away on the beach, but they couldn't think, couldn't remember exactly, because they were out past the waves and didn't watch him leave, and because their mom hadn't stopped crying, and the sun was getting low, and it was getting harder to remember and harder to pretend.

When they searched the beach for hours, they walked the sand and dunes. When they searched the water for days, they looked, and they listened, and they called.

When the week was over, they stayed at the cottage and waited. When two weeks were over, they stopped waiting and simply stared. When summer was over, they had to leave somehow. When they packed their things, their mom stopped talking altogether.

When they finally left for home, the seagull watched them go.

LA STREGA RAGNA

PAZIENZA. SHE'D GROWN TIRED OF THE MEAT AND MARROW of over sugared children. Or maybe just her body had.

She'd grown tired of cleaning this oven too. On that her body agreed. Her knees were too bony for kneeling and her fingers too fat for scraping, but Uvetta did it because there was no one to help. Cobblestones lined the oven floor. They made sense a hundred years ago. And they looked good, not that anyone ever saw them until it was too late. Still, it was an infernal chore to clean the oven. She chuckled at her own joke. Ran her tongue over her dentures. No snaggle teeth for her. Reaching all the way back, she scraped the ash forward. A small piece of bone was in the mix; Uvetta brushed the ash off it. Tossed it aside. Too small to wash in the sink and suck the marrow out. She continued to scrape, her metal trowel screeched against the oven floor; her doctor's advice bounced around her brain.

She rose to her feet, did a few of the prescribed yoga moves. Downward facing dingbat that her doctor was, he'd remarked at her agility for her age. If he only knew. She was here when the tales were true and beasts roamed the forest.

None as beastly as her, of course. Fierce and patient. It isn't everyone with the power to let dinner come to them. Spin a little web, spin a little more. Wait for the children to come to the door.

It was delicate, and powerful, and that's what she liked about it. None of this outright aggression, just a simple invitation. What to do now. What to do now that her doctor insisted her diet change. Over-sugared children were wreaking havoc with her insulin levels or some such diabetes nonsense she found hard to believe. Or she would have, if she hadn't felt the dizziness herself, seen her vision go double. And then of course, there was the added problem of supply and demand. If kids were already eating all that sugar, what did they need with her little cottage of delights and desserts in the woods? She could buy food, and of course she could grow food. But she *liked* eating children. And at her age, shouldn't she be able to eat what she wanted?

Uvetta stood in her doorway to give her knees a break and take in the forest air. Fresh and clean, and unfortunately empty of humans. No matter, she'd think of something soon. She broke off the tiniest piece of peppermint from the door jamb, sucked it slowly. It had no taste. Unlike the children of course, and with that, a craving tightened her stomach and her saliva pooled. Children. Fat and sugar. Meat marbled with glistening white, grown crispy in her oven and filling the cottage with its delicious scent and an occasional whimper. "Cut out red meat," the doctor said. She could only assume that included children. Sure, she could feed on birds and beef, but why do that when their beaks and blood brought her the truly tasty. Spin a little web, spin a little more.

Who was she kidding? She hadn't seen a child in these woods in years. The peppermint was stale in her mouth, and she spit it into the dirt. Her fingernail picked at the edges of the door while she thought, and thought, and the leaves lifted off the ground and swirled in response, danced and dashed. No matter. No matter. She'd been here before, hadn't she? She'd been here when everyone else was running around catching children, dragging them, screaming and crying. That was no good, and not just because it brought villagers running. That was no good because it ruined the meat. She hadn't understood the science of it until she caught wind of two ranchers talking, discussing the calves and how if they were stressed, the tender meat became tough. They were a mountain range away but it wasn't hard to hear when you really listened. She did a taste test. On the filet, not the ranchers. Went into the village one day, ordered mignon, extremely rare. The waiter pretended that was a problem, but she adjusted his thinking. She was changing minds long before light sabers and droids roamed the universe. True enough, the meat was tainted from the terror. It was as she suspected all along. Chasing the children scared them, scaring them ruined the taste.

Still what to do? She left the cottage and drifted into the village for a look around. She wandered, invisible the way all women are, past a certain age. Just as well. She resented being there but given the state of her house and its utter failure to attract, it was necessary to walk among them. No one spoke to each other, never mind her, and every single child, delicious though they may be, had their face stuck to a cell phone. That was a serious spell, Uvetta thought, and she shuddered to think of the witch that created those little relics. Every single human was bound, so much so she couldn't make eye contact long enough to cast a thing. Frustrating. Unhealthy or not, she needed to eat. And more importantly she wanted to eat. Children. Even one child. A small one, like an appetizer. That was a thought, perhaps she could manage her health through portion control. She imagined tiny fingers and toes, laid out in neat rows on her serving platter. Followed immediately by an image of her gorging herself on the rest of the body, eyes last of course for dessert. Absurd. One child to tide her over, until when?

Uvetta caught a breeze back home and stared at the oven. Could have it done in twenty minutes of course, but there was nothing to do after that. That was the problem no one ever talked about – if there's an incantation for everything, the satisfaction just isn't there. Nothing to do and no one to eat. Maybe she'd get a place in town. Something near the playground. Those kids had to be at least slightly healthier, what with the running around. Sweaty though. And probably on security cameras. She'd never show up on film, but public harvesting was never her style. There had to be a way.

Time to ask the universe, as the humans liked to say when they pretended to understand such things. Uvetta whispered to her mixing bowl, ran a finger around the edge before she added eggs, flour, and water bit by bit. Rolled the dough on the bed and cut it into long strips, telling it stories, tales of lost items found, families reunited, and always, always delicious feasts, as she crimped the dough into ridges and ruffles. Back to the kitchen. Layered the noodles, the stories, the cheese, the need. Mozzarella, ricotta. And the sauce of course: pomodori, basilico, oregano. A few extra ingredienti whose names she never spoke. Lasagna. Deliziose sì sì sì. Lasagna went into the convention oven— the walk in was strictly for humans because she liked the children to smell the ones that came before as they burned and bubbled. Speaking of, the mozzarella on top was bubbling nicely. Lasagna really was the most comforting of spells. Layered. Cheesy. Hearty enough for the effect to travel miles and miles with just a hint of spice in the sauce and even better when frozen and reheated. No time for that. She ate a portion herself and left small portions on her windowsill to be picked up by the others. She couldn't see them of course, anyone who says they can see the others is lying. But she heard them, as they drifted over in pairs and small groups, trying to act all casual, and then snatch! They grabbed a piece and it swirled away, gone, gone, gone to do her bidding hopefully, to do theirs some of the time. The spirits she called on weren't entirely reliable and had no manners whatsoever. Not so much as a thank you.

"You're welcome!" she called.

It was so fast she couldn't be sure she made it happen. The low rumble of a truck pushing itself, the motor whining on the far side of the trees, and then all of a sudden it was in front of her, pulled up nearly at her doorstep. Well, that was quick. There were three of them, and she really wasn't that hungry, so she took her time deciding who to eat. All male; how boring, the one with excessive facial hair was out immediately. She wasn't going to pluck someone at her age. One had a cigarette dangling and she could smell the disease already in his lungs. It's such a pain in the ass when you buy fruit and it expires by the next morning. And the third, well the third wasn't going to do anything for her new fat free diet. Uvetta groaned and thought about the stories she'd whispered. Had she been specific enough? It wasn't like her to have something backfire like this, could it actually be a coincidence? The wind ruffled her hair in response. Ah. She had to listen.

The men spoke of many things as they took pictures and measurements and looked around the site. It was odd that they were here at all, technically there was no road. She lost any thought of lunch as she watched them. Men of this age generally tasted like shit. It wasn't their fault, they had lived with so much testosterone for so long, it was like those calves for the filet mignon. If you're all jacked up all the time, high levels of "gotta do gotta be make it happen king of the world"... well, ruins the meat.

They were going to build a tower it seemed. For the cell phones. Excellent, she remembered towers, she'd locked enough children in them. No tower at the moment. Just a candy-coated two bedroom with a wrap-around porch and a view of the valley. Sure, the architecture of the house changed over the years, not that it mattered. They only saw it if she wanted them too. A little nook for reading. And the kitchen stayed the same through the centuries. Walk-in ovens take forever to season but the deep human flavor was worth it. Uvetta was very particular about that.

Still, she was so hungry; it was a tough decision, to let them go, to let them build. But she knew the terrain was rocky enough that they would never be able to build anything more than this tower, even if she let them. And only the fittest, most accomplished hikers would make it this far, thereby solving her fatty tissue problem. Well. This is why she'd survived this long, outlived her sisters, outlived the demoni that tried the sewers, the attics, all the peopled places. La strega ragno was as patient as she was fierce. It took weeks for the cell tower to come together. She floated up to the ridge and watched them work while her stomach rumbled. It was a terrible version of a tree, she couldn't believe anyone would be fooled, or that anyone but her would care this far off. Still. They did the work for her, and in exchange she let them walk away each day. It felt like cheating, a little, not to spin her own web.

And what a web they wove for her. A strong connection, full bars in her front yard. Uvetta knew they'd come— hikers, and maybe, just maybe a family or too. Who could resist? Full bars in the middle of a forest. She made sure to say thank you to the others on the day it was finished. As she cleared the empty lasagna plate from the windowsill, she left a drop of blood in its place. Not that it solved everything. The hikers would likely be too healthy to keep around for long. The possibility of them escaping or hurting her was real so she wouldn't have a servant like she did with the children. But she would have a food source walking by her door, and that was enough. With a creak, she slowly bent her knees and knelt again in front of the oven. She reached as far as she could, all the way back to the furthest corner, and slowly scraped metal against stone to bring the pile of ash right up to her nose. What's this? A nibble of bone, a bit of a kneecap with the tiniest piece of tendon attached. She placed it on her tongue like a lozenge and sucked thoughtfully. Pazienza.

TO THE MOUNTAINTOP

Jack and Jill went up the hill to fetch a pail of water
    Jack fell down and broke his crown and Jill came tumbling
after.

— NURSERY RHYME

THE BUS LURCHED TO THE SIDE AND THE GIRL BUMPED HER head against the window. The babble of voices hiccuped for a moment, then shrieked and laughed and settled back into a high volume mix of music, insults and bravado. They were nervous, that was clear. It wasn't the great outdoors, per se, technically they lived in the suburbs not an urban concrete-scape. It was the uncertainty of what the coming trek held. What did it mean to climb a mountain? Bottom to top and back again. They were all older than the girl, and yet their fear fueled the shouting. Old enough to climb, bottom to top and back again. She was just there for the ride, for the hike, for the fresh air. And because the woman couldn't leave her alone. At least today there was a companion. A little girl named Lisa. Lisa was too small for ten years old not that time cared, or Lisa for that matter. She sat next to the girl, sucking on the sleeve of her windbreaker. Boredom or neurosis, it was hard to tell, and it didn't matter to the girl anyway. She was looking forward to the trees. Lisa looked like she was looking forward to the Vitamin D. And a retainer.

The ride was smooth until then, but the access road to the base of Mt. Lafayette had the ruts and bumps familiar to roadways that weren't regularly plowed. No ski lifts here that needed easy access, and there were no winter trails. When the snow melted, it left its own divots and gaps, hollow places big enough to catch a bus tire. The bumps became more frequent, but she was ready for them and her head held its own, away from the glass.

They finally rumbled to a stop and thirty faces pressed briefly to the windows before their owners hollered to get off get off get off the bus already. She was still making her way down the aisle when the first teens accidentally fell into the creek. It was too shallow to matter, but wet enough to draw concerned looks from the woman. Wet tees would not do for a youth group here to shout praise from the mountain top. The girl looked around for the leader, and saw him sitting off to the side, carefully wrapping the Book in a cloth, making a neat bundle and placing it in his day pack. He was muscular and tan in shorts and hiking boots and looked more likely to kick ass than praise and preach but she enjoyed the dichotomy. She glanced quickly around for the woman, who'd be horrified not only by her assessment of the leader but by thinking a word like dichotomy. Little girls were not supposed to be smart after all. At least, not smarter than the people who looked after them.

The woman herded the older children together, teens really, and went over the rules, which amounted to "Do Not Have Fun." She then turned proceedings over to the leader who, the girl was shocked to see, read from the Book right there in the open, right there on the earth. Her disquiet sent a rumble through the trees, a sharp breeze that drew the attention of the woman, so she quickly calmed herself to consider - *what was this?* The Book was limited to the building, why bring it here, why disrupt the trees. They were definitely disturbed, she felt an ache move through her, but finally he stopped. Closed the Book. And then they hiked.

They began their ascent, and to her delight, she found Lisa to be an excellent companion, in that neither kept to the trail, neither kept in sight of the leaders, and neither particularly cared where they went, as long as it was up. Feeling free was too rare for her to consider slowing down, and soon she and Lisa were far ahead of the loud, and already complaining, group. They scrambled over rocks, weaving in and out of the marked trail, stopping to splash in a small waterfall, cold water painfully good in their throats. It took the better part of three hours and they probably doubled the distance by wandering, but no matter. She vaguely knew the way the others would take – up to the summit, across a ridge to Mt. Lafeyette and down the trail again. The trees sang as she ran, and she was close enough to drift her hand across the quivering bark and let them know, yes, she was near, yes, she was with them. Yes, she was home.

The two girls approached the summit, and the trees shrank, too scraggly to push back against the wind which tore across the ridge and swept the granite bare. The path disappeared, so they skipped round and round boulders dropped like forgotten dice. They settled out of the wind against the far side of an outcropping, right on the edge of a sheer drop off. She was happy to see Lisa didn't flinch at the height, just pressed her back against the rock and slid down until she was seated. A paper bag held a flattened peanut butter and jelly sandwich, an apple, and a warm soda, which they split after it exploded. Lisa held it out over the edge, foam dripping down her hands and dropping too far to see.

On the far side of the summit, the rest of the group wandered up and collected themselves on a series of natural ledges, benches almost, pulling off boots and sneakers to examine and then squeeze blisters, squealing at the pus and liquid and chasing each other with dirty band-aids and sweaty socks, balled up and sailing over the edge into the forest below when they missed their targets. Lisa and the girl watched them from their own little ledge, watched them as the woman brought them back together, asked them to sit, asked them to please, please, please quiet down. Her voice drifted over the bare rock and faded just as it reached them. A distant call, disconnected.

Below the group, on a ledge of his own, the leader took a canteen out of his pack and carefully washed his hands. He paid no attention to the teens, now seated but shoving each other, and then they suddenly fell quiet as he unrolled the bundle holding the Book, placed the wrapping on the flat table of rock in front of him. He paused, and held the Book high, before placing it on the fabric and opening it to read. The girl watched him, head bowed, voice rumbling, not a moment, not a glance for the ridgeline of the mountains spread behind him. And still, he insisted on speaking. Back to the hills, just a setting a backdrop really for his verse and veil, his preach and pray. She stared and felt the dust begin to swirl past her feet, the wind snap through Lisa's jacket and tumble the smaller rocks. The trees dressing the mountains behind him picked up the message, rolled it around like wine. Turn around. Turn around around around around around turn around turn around turn around turn around turn around around around around around around around around turn around around around around around around around around around around around around turn around.

Her hands were stretched out, buried deep in the rock in front of her and firmly anchored and Lisa, she realized with a start, Lisa's arms were wrapped around her leg to stop from sliding any closer to the edge. The girl looked over at the leader, now standing with his back to everyone, no, not his back, just his head, twisted on his neck. It was comical, really, which is probably why those in attendance started to laugh, and then started to scream. The woman, eyes closed in prayer, opened them to see his head as it came back around to rest briefly on his shoulders and start a new revolution.

Looking down at her companion, the girl saw her hunched around her leg squeezing the last of the peanut butter and jelly sandwich. Lisa's mouth dropped open and a chunk of wet bread fell to the ground at her feet. Eyes wide, she watched the revolution of the leader's head, which showed no signs of stopping. Lisa closed her mouth, looked straight up at the girl and smiled a crooked, crooked smile. The girl relaxed, the trees let the wind fly away, and she slid her hands from the rock, no worse for wear.

Turning back to the crowd, she watched the leader, whose head was back where it belonged, face forward on a body hunched over the slab of granite, retching. She listened as the woman reassured the crowd, told them, *it's nothing it's nothing it's nothing*. They wiped snot off their noses and it was fine, shuffled closer together and it was fine; their hysterical sobs ebbed away over the mountain tops and it's fine it's fine it's fine. Over and over, over and over, until they believed, it's fine, and the leader rubbed his own neck and shoulders and believed, it's fine over and over and over it was nothing it was nothing it's fine *it's fine it's fine fine fine fine fine*. Until the impossible was invisible. And they could no longer see what they'd seen. And then the girl understood. Unlike the trees, they could be convinced. They could forget. They could hold evil in their eyes and not believe it.

Lisa's sweaty hand touched hers, and the girl felt her rise to kneel beside her, felt Lisa gently turn her hand to kiss her palm. Without looking down, she gently brushed her hair with her hand. Pressed her thumb into Lisa's forehead. A benediction. A promise. And then she pushed her off the cliff.

The woman walked ahead of him into the trees. Her footfalls soft and silent. No need to take off her shoes, but she went barefoot anyway the moment she entered the shadows. Leaned against a tree, pulled her sandals off and dropped them. She felt the earth, cool and quiet against her soles, against her soul, pine needles held her feet as she stepped down the path. The trees were whispering again— majestic, huge— and she breathed in deep, deeper to fill the space inside. Forest bathing, the lady at the hotel called it. She called it coming home.

You walk behind her, admiring her ass. She doesn't talk much, she never has, but that's what you like about her. Every time you try to recall her voice everything gets murky and you feel short of breath. That could be the trail.

Forest bathing. What kind of hippy dippy thing is that? But it's fine, it was time to get away for a few days, away from the city, from the wife, from the kids. You try to remember if the kids are still living at home but the air seems to take your thoughts away along with your breath. You met the woman at a bar, same as the others. But she was different. There was a ring around her, a space, like the crowd couldn't quite touch her. Was she hot? Maybe. Whenever you try to think of something specific, like the first time you took her, it all... fades. You know you took her, you take them all. But when you try to pull the memory up, try to pull up an image of her naked, begging... all you can see are her eyes from that night. You looked at her from across the bar and her eyes turned and locked on you. And then it goes faint. You know you slept with her because you heard her in the shower in the morning in your apartment. Not the one you share with your family, the one you share with the ones your family doesn't know about. Again, you pry your memories for something distinct, her body, or her touch, anything that tells you you know her. You remember following the sound of her into the bathroom, she was in the shower. There was steam, but the only thing you remember are her eyes. Her eyes.

You rub your chest. The hike must be getting to you. The idiot at the hotel said it wasn't a hike, just a walk, a way to forest bathe. Please. This is absurd. We should be back in the room fucking. And a voice in your head asks you, *Do you think that's what happens? Are you sure?* You shove it away because of course you screw her. Screw them all.

She walks ahead of him, just slightly out of range, and she starts to blur around the edges. The trees have so much to tell her and the earth is begging, begging for her so she moves quickly to the far side of a grove and presses her face against a tree. It welcomes her, remembers her. She peels off her dress to get closer and the bark scratches memories into her skin.

· · ·

You lost her. For Christ's sake, she's gone. One minute she's on the trail ahead of you, and now she's gone. Well, she couldn't have gotten far. You don't bother to hurry, the trail is easily marked, it's not like you could get lost. Just to be certain, you look back the way you came. There's still some light in the distance, so you know where the lodge is. Forest bathing, the pamphlet said. Well, fine. You owed her that much. You stop to rest against a tree, press a hand against the bark and a flash of pain pops behind your eyes, pressing against them and you see her, in your mind, you see her flesh spread out on your bed and a deep tattoo, ingrained in her skin. It had to be a tattoo. It had to be. But it felt like bark. And that's just not possible.

The woman almost forgot about him, face pressed against her tree, listening to the stories until she felt the heat of his palm on her skin. He was touching them, and they were not happy.

You see her then, just up the trail. She's naked, and no shit, she's hugging a tree. It's too much. It's nearly almost too much. Mind blowing sex or not this is ridiculous what would they say back— no. They'll never know. Same as always. You fucked her brains out, that's all anyone needs to know. A shiver slides down your spine and slips under your balls, cold and clammy. She's just a girl. Hugging a tree for fucks' sake. She's hugging a tree. This is not normal. You gasp, rub your chest the pain is a little tighter and she turns her head. Eyes straight at you. And you can't see anything else— your feet are stuck in your boots your boots are stuck to the ground it's happening again, the fog is coming and you fight it, fight it harder as it turns to smoke, hot and dry.

· · ·

She pressed her palms against the tree and let her fingers sink through the bark, past the thick outer edge past the present and into the memories she pushes deep, deeper, deeper to the scars. Ah. She starts to cry, feels the fingers of a fire licking at her skin, holds the memory of that pain as it covers her.

You can't breathe. The smoke is pushing itself up your nostrils forcing its way into your lungs. You can't breathe. You haven't taken a breath in minutes, maybe days, you won't take the smoke in but it doesn't care; it forces its way into your body, you feel the flames licking your feet, curling around the skin of your calves coloring it smoky gray then black, finally pink as it splits open to reveal new flesh that smokes and crisps and dies, burns and splits to reveal new flesh, smokes splits dies again. Open your mouth to scream and suck the smoke deep into your lungs; it crawls into all the spaces you didn't know you had you are full you have to be full there can't be space anymore inside you for any of it when your stomach starts to boil. Organs too hot to touch touching each other, you shouldn't be able to tell where the edges are the blood screaming into steam and vessels bursting the contents of your stomach erupt into your abdomen burning acid and flames taking you right down to your skeleton she puts the story into your soul, patches you over with new skin and sends you on your way.

She remembers. She listens and she remembers. As she pulls her arms back out of the tree, she turns to the man. He holds a layer inside him now, a layer of ash and pain, an archive of fire. She will touch him again. When the time comes.

CHAT BOX

> There's something in the closet...
> There's something under the bed...
> There's something in your dreams...
> There's something that's dead...
> There's something coming closer...
> There's something after you...
> There's something in the air...
> There's something in your shoe.

MCKENZIE LAUGHED. OOH, SCARY. THE SHOE LINE GOT him every time. He heard the chant floating over from the school playground; the kids were outside, yelling, laughing, running, laughing some more. He envied them the freedom. Now that he was free, he envied them that

feeling

of

release—

There's something in the closet...

He stretched his arms out in a classic V, pushed his back over the top of his desk chair until he heard his spine pop, then collapsed in on himself to contemplate his day. So much time left until sundown. He heard a bump from the closet and paused... nothing. His message light blinked, and he logged back in to help Mrs. Widdlemeyer from Tuscon with her rental. Terribly sorry, Mrs. Widdlemeyer, that you were upset at the ending of a movie about the Titanic. We feel like the title should have clued you in, you fucking moron.

<delete> <delete> <delete>

He erased the truth and wrote something bland and pleasant until Mrs. Widdlemeyer felt he solved her problem.

Thump, thump, thump from the closet.

No matter.

The lock

would

hold.

There's something under the bed...

After two hours of pointless, pre-written chatter that all ended with...

> **...Is there anything else I can do for you today?**
> **...Here's a survey link to report my ~~utter apathy~~ service.**

...he turned off the monitor and took his coffee out to the back yard. Gave the rhododendron the last dregs of it and waited. The children were quiet, they must have gone back inside. Recess over. He made a sandwich and settled back at his desk. The east coast was after sundown so the calls about interrupted service would be fast and thick. Devastating, to have your movie interrupted you see. Absolutely mind blowing. Late afternoon he took another twenty-minute break and walked upstairs to his bedroom. He could see it under the bed as he came up the steps. It was probably a feng shui issue, having the bed directly in front of the door like that, but there was really nowhere else to put it. And he liked seeing it come into view under the bed as he came up.

First step

second step

third step

nothing.

Fourth step just a peek of the wrapping, tight and lumpy. Fifth step he could catch most of it but not all. Sixth step was too far so he'd gotten in the habit of lingering between the fifth and sixth to view as much of it as possible at once. And the form under the bed twitched as his footstep hit the creak on the sixth, so that was an added bonus.

Step

creak-twitch.

Step

creak-twitch.

Giggle.

There's something in your dreams...

He had time for a little siesta before he jumped back online. He knew the bed would just touch it as he lay down, so he was very, very careful. And he knew it was holding its breath, because he was. Slowly lowering himself, he felt the sink of the mattress and the smallest breath escaped from underneath. It may have been his imagination, but he could swear he felt its breath swirl around his ankles. He lifted them quickly and tucked them up into his chest.

Naptime.

Quiet now.

There's something that's dead...

Peckish. He woke up peckish, not hungry, not not hungry. He popped open the freezer to grab a little something. The smell was undeniable, so he must not have frozen it properly. They were difficult to take care of after a while. Unlike some, he was not averse to euthanasia. In fact, he was verse to it. Was that a word? It should be. The stench was going to be a problem, so he unwrapped the foil and let the remaining ooze go down the disposal. It crunched a little, but less than you'd think. It was sad, sometimes, when they were done. Not always, some of them were more bother than they were worth,

but still.

He missed them

in his way.

There's something coming closer...

It was almost time. That was the pain and the delight of it all, wasn't it? It was almost time, and then it would be time, and then it would be over, and he would have to wait again. He never felt the urge to speed time up and slow time down as badly as the hour before sunset. But it didn't matter, did it? Because he was free, and tomorrow he would still be free. So perhaps he was just creating these little traps in his own head, these little ways to be released.

. . .

There's something after you...

There were three messages waiting when he got back downstairs. He opened the chat with each of them, and then played a game he liked to call, 'how much can I piss you off before you click on the little x.' His favorite part was to offer the solution to someone else's problem instead of what he knew would help, just copy paste the same answer around. It didn't matter, they thought he was a bot anyway. He liked to watch them get frustrated, once the video software kicked in. Sometimes it took a while, sometimes they had something stupid like a piece of tape over the camera and then it didn't work at all. That used to make him so angry, but now, now it didn't really matter. He kept his favorites open in a folder, and the rest, he just helped and sent along their merry way.

...Anything else I can help you with today?
...Thank you. Please give me five stars.

There's something in the air...

It was getting colder, and that was good. People tend to pay less attention when they are hurrying to get somewhere. Collars up, hats down, heads hunched into their shoulders against the wind. Easier to help. Easier to follow, not too closely, and wait for the inevitable slip on the ice and then 'Are you all right? Oh yes, thank you. Are you sure? It looked like you twisted your ankle. I'm an EMT, do you mind if I check?'

He never said doctor,

or cop,

or nurse.

There's something in your shoe.

It was nothing to ask, "Does it pinch?" as he gripped the

ankle in his hand. If it didn't already he made certain it would as he crushed the bones between his fingers. A gasp, always. Surprise, always. It was nothing to squeeze with hands so strong, as his fingers tried to connect never mind there was a person, flesh over sinew over bone in between. It was nothing to catch them as they drooped, as they mumbled yes, and he was delighted when they managed a note of surprise through the haze. No one expects pain that sharp, no one expects the dizziness, the nausea that comes when the body is overwhelmed. The needle slipped from his pocket, a quick puncture then, above the break where they didn't feel it. Couldn't feel it compared to the pain radiating up from that ankle as solid bone turned not liquid but shattered. A shifting puzzle. Nothing to see. Nothing but prompt service. He held the dear ankle as he looked around for anyone else who could help, anyone else who could care. Shortly, the moaning started, sometimes vomiting and so forth. It was nothing to worry about, he said, it was nothing. But, just in case, would you like me to help you? And if they said yes, and they always said yes, who was he to leave someone in need? His job, his entire existence, was customer service.

And
he
aimed
to
please.

How can I help you today?

THEIR VOICES WHISPERED, AN UNDERLYING CURRENT OF soft wounds, murmured without inflection just below the surface. His voice took flight across the room—skimmed across the crowd to roll up the far wall and wash back over her again, settle into her, surround her, support her. She seemed to float in place, there at the back of the room.

His words.

His words returned to his mouth where he drank them in and swallowed her whole. She stood with the crowd to face him, but there was no light shining from on high, no glow from his eyes. That's fallacy, that's the stuff of fairy tales. This was real life. And it was finally happening to her. The lights in the hall were muted and she felt the press of bodies around her, the perfume of excitement and fear rolled over her in waves, mixed with her own adrenaline, close and heavy, lifting her heart and grounding her feet. They swayed a little, every time he spoke, a roll of energy that washed over them, and she stretched upward in response and sank as it passed. Her eyes glittered. She was with her kind, her kindred. She imagined them as a school of fish, moving and flashing together, stronger together, slipping around obstacles. And they were the only ones who understood. It had taken so long to come to this, so long to be here with them. She pressed onto the balls of her feet to try and see the front but there were too many people, and the guy with the drooping mustache elbowed her to stay in place. She smiled at him. Today was a good day. Today they were going to the island, and it was going to be so beautiful. She tried not to imagine it, didn't want to get carried away on a dream. Focused. She squeezed her hands into tight fists and released them, slowed her breathing.

If Jody looked through the crowd, she knew she'd see lips moving slightly, like watching fish breathe through the wall of an aquarium. Mouths popping open and closing, lips wrapped around words holding ideas formed into facts solid enough to stand on, firmly, two feet and her face raised high. A frenzy wouldn't do, not for her. This was slow and deliberate and powerful. She felt powerful, for the first time. She felt strong. Not just in her body, that was easy. She felt like she was doing the right thing at the right time. She knew it was real, it was all really happening and yet it also felt like that fairy tale, one with a prince. The way she found him. Or he found her, that's what he said. He'd been waiting for her, he'd been hoping for her, searching for her, only she could make him feel that way, only she could love and support him. No one else understood. She was a little surprised, the first time she came to a meeting, offended even, at the crowd, at the mass of people there. But now she could laugh at herself. Of course. He would have so many who loved him. Of course. Like scales locked one over the next, slipping around the body of a fish. It soothed her, to be one of many, smoothed away her doubt. Her brain twitched as that doubt rose again, always ready to strike from the depths. She rolled her shoulders, cracked her neck. No place for that. No place for even a hint of that here. She glanced around. No one noticed. No one saw the waver in her belief even as she imagined it leaping over her head, signaling her location, pointing her out to the true believers before it sank again.

"Prepare yourself!" he said, his voice ringing out. She still couldn't see him, but she imagined him looking out, excited by so many, by their faces, their presence, their adulation. She'd never slept with him, but she'd heard the rumors. 'All talk and no cock' was the general consensus. And frankly that was fine; they were there for more important things and she had no interest, no need of distractions. But she knew, they all knew, what had happened in service to that cock, and how very likely it was that he was excited, even now. On today of all days. Well. No one was perfect. It didn't show of course, and it would have been overshadowed by his great drooping belly even if it had. She wasn't young enough to be asked to pledge; she'd known that the moment she saw his handlers, blonde and deceptively bland. Blank eyes. Sharks. Men weren't asked to pledge unless they were leaving, then they were bent over until they bled and left somewhere to be found. Or not. And no one truly left, not really. Not in the sense that they renounced him or the way. One day they were in the circle, and the next they weren't.

She felt a wave of shame for thinking about things that were not her concern. She realized she'd spent far too much time already thinking about something so inconsequential, so she squared her shoulders again, shifted her feet. And that's when she noticed it. The woman standing to her left turned slightly toward her and there, there it was. The mark. She drew her breath in sharp and felt mustache man turn to her. He must have seen it too then, over her shoulder. A mark. Here. In this room. Mustache man pushed up close against her and pressed past, driving his fist into that face, into the mark. She heard teeth crunch and blood flung across her arm, across the backs of the people in front of them. Then Mustache was kicking her, whoever she was, down on the floor with the blood pooling around her head. A few people turned around briefly, then gave their attention back to the front. There were instructions. The time was near. Another woman started toward the body, grabbed its arm and started to pull it back to its feet when she saw the mark on its face. She stopped and dropped it back to the cement, a low thud. Stepped on the hand as she walked back to her spot, tried to catch up in the hymnal. The hand twitched and lay still, twitched and lay still, as Mustache kicked its owner in the head until it broke open, showed a soft pink mound graying in the air. He grunted then, walked back to his place on the other side of her. She felt bad for him, they had a long journey ahead and it probably wasn't wise to expend so much energy. Well. His path was his business.

It was the last time they would all meet in this way. After this, only the true believers would make it to the island, only the chosen. She wondered if she'd see Mustache again, or the woman who tried to help it stand before he crushed it. Eyes front, she rolled onto the balls of her feet one last time and yes!— caught a glimpse of his face between the heads and shoulders just as he said "Go," and he smiled, "I'll be with you." Yes. Yes. He spoke directly to her, and she knew she would see him there, on the island. She would make it. All the way. A small voice cried out, the briefest call, and her head jerked around instinctively, looking for the bird. She remembered these birds, these black birds with shiny feathers that would sit on the wire outside her house and squawk and squawk. Huge numbers of them, scattered across the lawns, talking at her endlessly as she ran errands or kept watch. It was absurd though, a bird in this room in the cellar of a skyscraper, and she was shocked to realize the sound was probably in her head. She cocked it to listen, but it didn't offer advice, just a whimper, an echo of the thing lying on the floor maybe. She looked at the hand again and sure enough, it twitched. She'd heard that, that your brain can keep trying to communicate with you even after the rest is disconnected. Or maybe it's the reverse, your body keeps going even when your brain doesn't work? What was wrong with her? She needed to focus. To prepare.

The boats were waiting, just like he promised. They were big and it was easy enough to line up. He had to go on ahead of course, he had other things to prepare. It's not like she expected them to take a bus together. Sit in the back holding hands, like a field trip. Would have been nice though. To have a moment alone with him again. Just to say thank you. Well, she'd show her gratitude by being the first one there. She'd prepared herself, swimming on the weekends. Of course, she wasn't going to beat the guy who'd competed internationally, but she knew she'd make a good showing. Maybe the swimmer would hold the door for her when they got to the island. And she would thank him on the way in. She heard that call again, the distant shriek of a bird, and she tried to think around it— the water, and then the island, and then there would be a door. The door would open. The door would open. She couldn't get past that part in her daydream; the shriek kept interrupting so she gave it up as a bad job and scanned the crowd. Maybe later, when everyone quieted down, she'd try again. Savor that moment she was so looking forward to. She twitched again, anticipating. Right now there were too many people bustling around. Everyone was polite, though the thrum she felt in the basement was diluted a bit out here in the big sky – closer to a party, or a picnic. Or a day at the beach. She smiled, walked across the sand at a comfortable pace. Had to conserve her energy. She saw Mustache again for a moment, as they boarded. He was off to the side, talking, and she saw the tiny earpiece. No wonder he'd acted so quickly back there, he was a professional too. Still, she was glad he handled it. He looked like he was breathing heavy from the effort. Or maybe he was still vibrating, still up from his activity in the basement.

Beautiful day, blue sky, warm sun. She considered the journey ahead and she smiled. Finally here. They were going to do this, together. They were going to be back where they belonged. Not that she'd ever been to the island, but she'd seen it in pictures. It took longer than expected to get to the drop off point out there on the water. All that day and night on the boat, waiting to arrive, waiting to start really. She slept, the kind of sleep that isn't restful, the kind that knows you're sleeping and won't shut up about it. About an hour before dawn the boat slowed, then stopped, then shuddered as the engines turned off. There were dozens, a whole fleet, seventy, maybe eighty she guessed. Decks packed, edges nearly touching each other, each one a universe and a single cell. Each one filled with people exactly like her, doing the right thing at the necessary time. Flags and banners and color splashed across the water, until the sun broke over the edge of the world and bleached them out. It was hot almost immediately. Time to get ready.

She slipped her sweatpants off and her top, her tight swimsuit already underneath, covering her from thigh to shoulder. She knew it didn't matter when you arrived, but like most people, she was so eager to get there, she'd thought about things like reducing drag in the water. The competitive swimmer, the one they all assumed would get there first, was shaving his head and his legs, and there was a brief scuffle between two guys who grabbed for his razor when he set it down, but in the end, they shaved each other, so it worked out. It was nothing, then, to smear the blood onto each other, coating their forearms, their thighs. She wondered for a minute if they were distracted, their thoughts on someone other than the one who was by now waiting for them on the island as she watched their hands slow and press and rub. But then she realized, that's exactly what she was doing, getting distracted. She closed her eyes, turned away from them as they painted each other's faces in thick red stripes, drying brown. There was a bucket of cow's blood nearby, and the woman smearing it across her chest looked like she'd be done soon. Stepping forward, Jody took her turn, careful to soak her hair, knowing from her trials at home that it could hold a lot of blood, willing to give up the aerodynamic advantage of a shaved head to gain a higher blood content on her body. She took care to rub it into her ears, knowing how well the crevices could hold conditioner found long after she took a shower, a blob of yellow crusting orange as the edge congealed into a rind, dry and flaky and easy to scrape out with her fingernail.

Another scuffle broke out over the ground beef, but she was no fool. She brought her own meat, pulled it out of her backpack. It was a real find that backpack, insulated and came with its own freezer pack. Still cold after... what had it been, two days since she left home? The meat wasn't frozen though, and it dripped onto the deck as she tied it around her waist, shoving chunks of calf liver into the pockets of her vest before she slipped it on over her suit. Again, tamping down her competitive instinct in order to follow the instructions to the letter. The more blood, the better, the more meat, the better. She knew she'd done it right when she saw the stares around her. Oh, how she wished she could share this, snap a pic, post it, watch the comments and the shares and the jealousy. But really what did they matter? They were on the boats with them or they weren't. And the only one who wasn't was the man who led them here, and he was waiting on the island. Now she couldn't wait, and she moved quickly through the crowd, used the swimmer striding forward as a blocker. He was taller than she was so she could easily drift into his wake and up to the front of the boat. The bow it was called, if she remembered right.

Suddenly, she was there, nothing but water stretching out in front of her. It was a few minutes after sun rise, certainly less than an hour.

She jumped.

The water was warmer than expected and she laughed as she came back to the surface. Just another lie she'd been told her whole life. Salt on her tongue, instructions echoed in her head: swim toward the sun. She dove under the surface and came up stroking, arms pulling through the water. Comfortable. Relaxed. She knew to keep her head down, so her chest would be level, swimming almost on the water rather than in it. The waves were small but still a little harder than expected; most of her open water training was in a lake. Perfect form, fingers together, hands cupped slightly, the pull of her arm through the water, a tight arc around her head pushing the water all the way to her hip and then reaching, reaching far overhead to pull her hand again through the water, propelling her forward. The muscles deep in her shoulders warming with the effort. Jody kicked from the hips only, let the rest of her legs relax behind her, saving them for when she needed to rest her arms. It was taking longer than expected when she felt the first bump on her ankle.

The instructions were specific, and she was so grateful they were, because she did get a little nervous after the bump, when she brought her head up and heard the screams from the others in the water. "Swim!" she heard from behind her, a voice calling through a megaphone, "Swim!" Think about yourself, the instructions said, as you swim think about what they took from you, think about what you need as you move toward what's yours. She needed to get to the island, but she took a glance back to see where the boats were, where the voice came from and just as promised, they were gone. She knew he wouldn't make it easy; he'd said it would be hard, that so many would get in their way. It was a sign of his faith in them, in her, when the boats were gone, it meant she was getting close. Swim. She put her head back down and swam, switching to breaststroke when her legs grew tired, using the strength in her shoulders now to pull the water towards her and behind. Towards her and behind until the dull ache was shoved from her mind by a cramp, sharp and sudden, in her thigh. Uncomfortable. Then another a little higher and she felt muscle tearing away but he'd said there was nothing in the water, laughed and said they had nothing to fear – they were chosen.

Her suit was too tight she was certain. It was a wardrobe problem. The edge, the elastic squeezing her thigh so hard it cramped, sudden and stabbing. She rolled her ankle, tried to work it out, tried to relax the whole leg while she continued to swim, willing herself through the water. Swim. Move forward. The island was getting nearer, she knew, because he said they would have to swim through the pain. Be strong he said. She would not float on her back to work out the cramp, as she knew some of them were. Your belly was weakness, everyone knew that. She sure as hell knew that since she watched her dad beat her dog to death, even as it rolled over, paws in the air. 'Don't back down,' her father said. And then, 'Ask that one to clean it up' as he gestured at her mother? A servant? Someone walking by cleaned the pile of fur and feces that was her dog a few minutes before. It might have been a servant, it sure as hell wasn't anyone who lived there, so a servant. Or a messenger. Some worker. The screech of that bird was back again in her head, muffled by the water this time but relentless, screeching over and over until it blended into one endless scream.

The pain in her leg spread to her stomach next, making

her nauseous. She focused on her stroke. Reach. Pull. Again. When she finally vomited heat and acid poured out of her into the water. Her body stopped without her permission and she reached down with her hand to feel the muscle, work out the cramp but it was gone, her thigh was gone, a gap below the tight line of her suit, above her knee. She stuck her head under then and tried to look but the water was too dark in the shadow of her body, even with goggles she couldn't see anything. She took a deep breath and stuck her head under again, waving away the fish that came to nibble on whatever used be in her stomach as it drifted down, milky.

Somehow the sun was up a notch when she surfaced, left leg kicking hard so she could tread, making up for the right leg that dangled and wobbled from the knee down no matter how hard she churned at the hip. Again, she resisted the urge to float on her back. She was no quitter. She switched to lay on her side instead, stroking with left arm and left leg as her fingers slid down from her hip to the edge of the gap, finger-tips eased around a fringe of sinew that wasn't supposed to be there, slipped into that space above her kneecap and pushed against the flesh, followed it until she felt bone. She brought her hand to her face, but it was clean—wet and bright and pale. She looked at the water around her, and sure enough, she was floating in a cloud of blood, but then again maybe it was just the meat. She quickly checked her ears, not even a gob of blood left, and now maybe, maybe this was hers.

As Jody pulled off her vest, she realized it was tattered, the meat gone. He knew they would need it, and he was right.

He was right.

She risked floating on her back to try and tie the remnants of her vest around that space; the space where her skin was gone and her muscle shredded, but sure enough it made her dizzy to be on her back. And then her shoulders relaxed, and she realized she could sleep, she could just drift off to sleep but no, that was exactly what they wanted and she knew then the island was the only option. The island was the only way to save herself so she kept swimming certain she would be the first. She flipped onto her stomach and used long strokes, propelling herself through the water until finally the water came further and further over her head, just as he said it would, just like he promised, and then she knew she could let go. She could let go, and the island would pull her home, down into the depths beyond the cameras and the non-believers. Her body betrayed her, as he said it would, a last kick to the surface of the water her lungs gasping, that damn bird screeching in her head until finally she felt herself move down. She must be directly over the island now. Down through the water, away from the lies, away from the shimmer on the surface.

DRILL

"A little wider, Dustin? Thank you, I'm going to rub this on your gums, so you won't feel the needle, okay? All right, just a little pinch now."

Dustin could see her eyes smiling above her mask, lines at the corners crinkled just enough to look friendly. Friendlier than the array of instruments on her tray but that's what happens when you let disease take hold. She pressed the tip of the needle into his gumline, already puffy from decay. Made sure the thin metal spike was no further in than needed, then pushed the plunger. He felt a tiny sliver of pain and then nothing.

"I'm just going to rub this and make sure it gets going quickly." She rubbed his gum line hard with her index finger, back and forth, the latex glove squeaking over tight flesh. "I'll be right back with the doctor, you just rest for a moment. You wear your sunglasses, the lights are pretty bright."

He heard her behind him, gathering and arranging and he pictured the silver instruments. What a fool to wait so long. Well it would all be over soon. He'd only closed his eyes for a moment and she was back with the dentist alongside, his eyes slightly less friendly.

"You may feel some pressure during this, but you shouldn't feel any pain, all right? If you do, just tell us." She smiled to herself, hearing patients attempt to speak with a mouth guard, a couple of hands and at least three instruments shoved inside their open gullets was always entertaining. But they became distressed so easily, the body odor coming off of this one was already pungent. No need to alarm him. It was all routine and he'd clearly already scared himself.

It was simple enough, the tooth was dead, or near dead, and needed to come out. That kind of rot meant a mother load of bacteria, and the organisms were already working to dislodge it from his mouth. So much so, that the dentist simply popped it out, and dropped it onto the tray. The smallest amount of blood and a thin strand of the root, anemic and slightly gray. She thought it funny, as she always did, that we have roots in our mouths.

Dustin was sent on his way after a joke about pulling a toy from the children's treasure box, and did he want his tooth for the tooth fairy? She heard him make his follow up appointment as she cleaned the room. All the waste from the tray went into the biohazard box. All the waste except the tooth, of course, which she slipped into her pocket and fingered for the rest of the day, annoyed that her latex glove was making it impossible to feel the tiny bit of flesh clinging to the rough underside.

One screaming toddler and a sullen teen to go before she could leave for the day. All would be well. Remarkable how fear turns people into cliches. Dustin wasn't afraid afterward, seemed quite pleased in fact. At least he would be until the numbness wore off. Still, she was happy to have a piece of him. She thought about her plans for that night as she scraped at the teen's teeth, rinsed, and scraped again. The toddler wouldn't let them get near her, and for that she was rewarded with a lollipop by her mother, who had an extremely active guilt thing happening. She could tell because the woman spent more time apologizing to the tyke for having to be at the dentist than explaining what was happening, which might have been more useful. Who was she to say? Her plans did not include going home to children or a wife or even a girlfriend. Alone was better right now. More time for projects. And this, she thought, picturing the tooth in her pocket as she scraped behind the front teeth of a teen too cool to show he was scared. She wasn't sadistic though, didn't "accidentally" jab him in the gums that way some of the others did. Didn't seem fair to add to their pain and anxiety, not when she was already getting so much in return.

She rolled the paper mat from the final tray of the day and dumped the contents, eager to get the gloves off once and for all. She hadn't even been able to sneak in a real touch, fingertip to tooth.

"Good night!" she called as she pushed the office door with her back.

"Happy Friday" the receptionist called out. That's right, it was Wednesday, her Friday. She paused to think about the days stretched ahead of her.

"Any plans?"

She paused in the doorway, let the heat from outside warm her a little after all day in the fake refrigeration. For some reason the office manager thought freezing patients would be more comfortable.

"Same old, same old."

"You're such a homebody."

"Truly. Good night."

"Night."

She picked up the pace and caught the number 5 bus at the corner as it headed west towards the park. Leaned her shoulder but not her head against the pole, swaying with the standing group in coordinated lurches and dips. Languages floated around her head; Ukrainian, Spanish, Japanese, Chinese, Algerian— a soothing buzz only found in cities. She stretched her back, careful not to intrude on anyone's space while she let her elbow creep out to the side to discourage 'accidental' bumps. It didn't take long in her dozy state, she barely noticed the squeak and grind of the door until they got to her stop and her head snapped up in recognition. She stepped out near the corner of Grove and Cole and headed up three doors. It was the ugliest building on the block, by far, but better to live in the ugly building and get to look at the pretty ones she always thought.

A quick run up the long stairs and she was safe in her flat. Alone. She dropped her bag to the floor and pulled off her scrubs when she remembered – the tooth. She pulled it out of the pocket and put it carefully on the counter next to the sink. It was pretty clean, but still, she polished it again with her own electric brush. Carefully avoiding the dangling root, she scraped every bit of roughness and smoothed it to a high polish. She reached with her left hand into the drawer and felt for the dental cement as she admired her tooth in the light over the kitchen sink. Something in the drawer shifted when she opened it and poked her fingertip. The tooth, her tooth, dropped out of her hand and she watched it bounce in the bottom of the sink and back out again, just a flash of white in the air before it came to rest on the floor under the cupboard. She took a breath. And then another for good luck. That was close.

Careful of where she placed her feet, she picked up the tooth and placed it on a napkin in the exact center of the counter. She bent over, and at eye level she could see bits of dust clinging to the edge, to the fleshy root. She filled a small bowl with water and placed the tooth inside it, allowing it to sink before gently swirling with her pinkie. The dust lifted, and the root floated a bit above the tooth, waving in the tiny ocean like sea grass. She let it soak before taking it out carefully – the root stretched a bit when it met the surface tension of the water and she was afraid for a moment it would snap – but the water let go and she placed it on a fresh napkin, a bit of cotton bandage to soak up the moisture. She turned her attention fully to the drawer and saw a pack of toothpicks spilled and spiky, which explained the poke. Her finger was fine. Her tooth was fine. She made a cup of chai tea while she waited for it to dry.

"All better?" she asked, as she removed the cotton and touched her new tooth with a dry finger.

"All better."

It was getting late, and even though she didn't have to work in the office tomorrow, she'd hoped to be done by now. Still, no reason to rush. She found the glue, extra strength epoxy and went into her bedroom. There it was. Her beautiful collection. Shining in shades of white, tiny bone against tiny bone, each one polished to perfection. She let her eyes roam over the rows it had taken years to collect. Hundreds. Maybe thousands. First her own, arguing with her mother because she didn't want the tooth fairy to get them. Then the others. So many. Sometimes, for fun, she counted them but she always lost track. She giggled as she looked for the perfect spot. It was getting harder and harder to find, usually something on the edges. She might need to add a new row soon. Hunting was part of the fun. Not all of it, mind you, that came later. But hunting for the perfect spot in row after row of her teeth soothed her and gave it all a sense of order. Each in its place. Finally, she saw a small divot in the surface of the collection, eventually they did crumble a bit, though it took years. This must have been one she'd stolen from the bio waste bin. No one cleaned them like she did. She measured the space with her eye and added a drop of epoxy to the underside then quickly pressed her tooth into place. The fleshy root trailed up the side, added the tiniest touch of pink to the row of gleaming teeth.

It needed time to dry, solidify its place in the rank and file. Still in her bra and underwear, she stripped and took a quick shower, just to get rid of the day. It took a while to dry her hair, but it was worth it to avoid the tangles in the morning. Finally, she was ready. She did a quick test on her newest tooth, a firm little push to make sure it wouldn't wiggle. It was resolutely in place. Unlike it had been in Dustin's mouth. She gave it a little kiss and laughed because of course she couldn't kiss one tooth without kissing a bunch. Her collection was now as wide and deep as a queen size bed; she'd purchased a wooden platform frame in fact, when it became clear that leaving them spread on the floor was no longer feasible. She used to have a cat that liked to play with them, but cats are weird after all.

She opened her nightstand drawer and took out a book and her mask. The book was just in case she felt like reading. Unlikely. Still naked after her shower, she slipped the mask over her head. It had been trial and error in the start, like with the bed frame, but the mask was cotton- thick enough that the teeth wouldn't leave marks. In the beginning, she'd been foolish and ended up with tiny divots in her face. Like she was a golf ball.

She knelt next to her bed and licked the edge, running her tongue back and forth over the ridges of teeth while her fingers slid and rubbed. Smooth and bumpy at the same time, it was so relaxing. She was certain that no massage could equal it, as she stretched her body out. It was delicious, to lie face down on her teeth, so many, and let them press into her flesh. Her mask covered everything but her eyes and mouth of course, so she could roll, or lie on her side, without any worries, without any imprints to give her away. Her arms didn't matter, because she wore long sleeves, and always had on gloves, so the bumps there were never seen. She reached over to her sound machine, and placed the button between two channels. The high pitched screeeee that came out sounded remarkably close to a drill, and she drifted off to sleep.

MOTE

DUSTIN DUSTS. IT MADE HIM LAUGH, AND THEN IT MADE him sad. Laugh because it amused him, sad because there was no one there to laugh with him.

It was a long process, and he started it new each night. He sat in the driveway, looking at the house he grew up in. Not in the sense that he lived in it as a child. In the sense that it was where he came into his own. Well. There are lots of ways to grow up he mused, as he ran his finger along the dash and collected a small pile of dust. Rubbed it between his fingertips until it was gone. May as well get started. As he walked toward the house, he stuck his tongue into the gap at the back of his mouth and felt the nub of gum where his tooth use to be. The flowers bent in the shadows lining the drive. He turned the knob without unlocking the door; no one came here anymore. No one. His feet didn't disturb the dust on the porch and he was careful never to wear sandals.

It was exactly as he left it, of course. A coffee mug next to the sink, a ring of black drudge dried and hardened in place. He turned on the tap and it sputtered, flinging drops of water into the cup. He placed it in the sink and turned to face the room.

They were all still there, still staring. Each painting accusing him of not moving fast enough. Never fast enough. "Shut up," he muttered, and grabbed a damp rag from where it hung over the faucet, cleaned his hands. "Just shut your damn mouths."

He began on the west side, where he could still see, the sun making a weak attempt but an attempt none the less. "Clean up, clean up, everybody everywhere," he hummed the little song they used at the bookshop to get the younger patrons interested in picking up after themselves. It didn't make it feel like less work. Not to him or to them. Ashes to ashes dust to dust. He wiped each portrait quickly, careful to avoid the gaze. The older portraits were harder, the paint and resin cracked and pulling dust into them, but he did it anyway. Ran his finger up and down, up and down. The dust clung to him, hugged him close. He paid no attention to it, until he came to the end. Took a deep breath, and looked into her eyes.

"Hello mother. Did you have a nice day?" a giggle jumped out of his throat when he realized he'd spoken aloud. He began in the upper left corner again. Ran his finger down the front of her portrait. He waited, gathered, held the finger up in front of his face. The dust clung to it, formed a neat little pad of grey, and slowly sank into his skin. He wasn't sure how much of him was dust now, it had been so long. When his finger was clean, he swiped it again, leaving a clean streak over the surface of the painting. He watched his skin absorb it. When she was finished, when he'd touched every part of the painting, he pressed his head against hers, forehead to forehead.

"Nice talking to you, but it's time..."

He turned away without finishing. She knew what came

next. He pulled off his shoes, peeled his socks into a ball. Arms out, on his back, soles of his feet on the floor. And then he waited. The dust began to gather around him, swirling into soft patterns. It was weirdly comforting and he was having trouble being scared.

His mind drifted back to the beginning, the first time...

"Shhh, there's no need to be frightened." Dustin heard her say it but it didn't make any sense. No one tells you that you shouldn't be scared unless you should be. And it's no way to greet someone at the door. The wind rattled leaves across the porch that day, but the air didn't enter. Didn't cross the line where she stood, just inside the threshold.

"Yeah, I'm here for the house cleaning."

"Excellent. They're ready for you."

"They? The agency said one house, only one."

"Oh not the house dear, the portraits," the woman waved him in as she opened a drawer and pulled out a pair of white gloves, "White glove treatment, right?"

"Of course, yes, we offer... we offer only white glove treatment."

"I'm so glad. They are very important, very special, to me."

Dustin turned to face the wall she indicated— it was covered with art, from top to bottom. Remarkably lifelike portraits, the kind of thing Picasso seemed to do for the fun of it just to prove he could. It was hard to believe they weren't photographs.

"The dust irritates them, you see."

Dustin scanned the wall – entirely portraits. Some were people he recognized, like the politician bloated and scared, or the film star whose name escaped him but her eyes— the artist captured that desperation, that need to be seen.

"Holy shit. I mean, it's an impressive body of work."

"I'm glad you think so." Her voice held none of the condescension usually reserved for him, an art major who worked in a book store. 'Couldn't hack it with the tough guy artists' his mom said when he dropped out, 'Has to hide in a book store.' As if there were groups of artists roaming the streets, gangs of tough guys wielding art brushes and charcoal sketchbooks. Then again, his mom did talk about "those gangs and their spray paint" ruining her city, but he was pretty sure she'd never make the connection to art, even if you chopped it out of a building, framed it, and put it up in a room painted white with a little paper square off to the side —Title: THIS IS ART, ASSH*LE.

Dustin laughed again, imagined the tour guide spouting, "Here we have the artist commenting on the viewer even as she speaks to the viewer, note the asterisk inside of the word asshole, it too resembles the sphincter blah blah blah blah blah."

The woman stared at him, waiting for him to stop amusing himself and get to work.

"Where would you like me to start?"

"Oh, have a look first, they're happy to be appreciated."

All but two frames held finished portraits, none of them smiling. The second to last was a blocked-out portrait of the woman, which didn't startle him as much as the last, a simple sketch of a jawline exactly like his own. His nose lightly ghosted above it might have been wrong, but the eyes. The eyes were unmistakably his even in this form, a few strokes of a pencil. He turned to ask the woman about it but stopped because her eyes were watering, tears spilling over the lids. Then she blinked and her eyes, her eyeballs began to shrivel — the moisture dried and the whites puckered and shrank, the sockets curled in on themselves like a drain sucking down a clog as it collapsed. He stumbled back against the portraits felt the jab in his shoulder from the corner of a frame. She didn't move. And as Dustin stared her eyes rolled back into place and focused on him again. A smile split her face. Perfect teeth. Her hand reached out toward him, offered the white gloves again. He felt his own hand covering his mouth and quickly put it down by his side, then back to his mouth then to his side, jerking it back and forth until he finally settled it on the back of a nearby chair. For a little support.

"What the hell—are you… are you okay? Your eyes, I saw, your eyes were… what was that?"

She smiled, "What did you see dear? What did you see?"

And he wasn't sure, what he saw, there in the slanting light from the window, dust swirling and dancing around her. Maybe it was a trick. An illusion. Maybe he was having some reaction from the dentist yesterday. He stuck his tongue back into the gap and wiggled it, just to remember himself. He took the gloves. He cleaned the paintings.

It was easier the next time, to clean them. Easier and easier to breathe in the dust, breathe in the ash. She stopped coming to the door to greet him, he found her in the corner looking out the window. She was fading, he could see that. Not like a photograph, or a leaf bleached in the sun. She was leaving in layers. The first was her hair, he found it curled into ropes, steel gray and thicker than he expected. That was the first time he worked without gloves. He picked it up but it wound itself around his hands and melted through his skin while he tore at it, tried to pull it off, but it was gone, or it was buried inside him. He ran from the house that day. But the next evening he was back, drove without thinking, found himself in the driveway staring at the house. Hair, and then nails. They fell off all at once as he cleaned— he heard a clatter on the wooden floor behind him and there they were — ten fingernails, ten toenails. They disappeared just as quickly into his palm as he scooped them off the floor. Her skin was slightly less dramatic, at least when it started. Flakes really, bits and pieces floating in the air, dusting the furniture when he came back the next day like a gentle snowfall. She was looking less and less like herself, of course, less and less like a person and he looked at her portrait when he left each night, watched it reassemble her.

It took a while, her skin— epidermis, endodermis. A layer of fat, thin on her arms, thicker across her belly, puckered in the line of the scar low on her abdomen but wide. It was a routine. Dust the portraits first. Then absorb whatever she'd shed overnight. He wondered if he should try to move her from the window, if anyone would notice the woman slowly evaporating as she looked at the street. And she did look, her eyes focused, shifted, always open, though he'd stopped trying to speak to her weeks before.

He said hello; he got to work. He dusted, made jokes to himself about how absorbing his work was, apologized though he was sure she couldn't hear. And then he left. After the skin and the fat, he wondered if her eyes would be next, but he found muscle fibers in a pile around her feet, a ragged ball of veins and arteries rolled up in the corner under the couch. Her organs gave him pause, but he handled each one gently, picked it up, cradled it in his arms, finally took his shirt off to make it faster, skin to skin. So to speak. Afraid if he didn't absorb her quickly enough it would hurt her somehow.

Her skeleton seemed like it might be a problem. There was really nothing for it but to strip down, gently take her in his arms, cradle her. She weighed nothing of course, all two hundred plus bones of her. He sat in the rocking chair, night after night, rocking her as her legs draped over his, reassuring her. He was there. He told her stories about his days at the bookstore as her bones thinned. The shoplifters. The serial readers who finished the first book there in the store before they decided if they wanted to buy the sequel as his skin whittled her away. It was harder and harder to leave every night, harder and harder to believe she'd be there at all the next. When her eyes dropped into his open palms, he knew it was almost done. But she was still there, he told himself, resting his head on top of hers.

Until she wasn't. One day he came, and there she was, on the wall. Complete. He stood for a long time, looking at her portrait, remembering her when she was all together. Placed his forehead against hers, and whispered for the first time, "Hello mother." He kissed her cheek.

Moved to his portrait on the wall, traced the outline of his shoulder, his neck, his collar bone. Stood in front of the empty portrait next to his, wondered who it would be. When he would make the first pencil strokes to call him, whoever he was, whoever was next. And he'd ask, like she did in the beginning when the work was done, "You'll come back though, won't you? You'll come back?"

He ran his finger over the soft fuzz on his upper lip.

"Yes."

INK

THE BELL CHIMED AND SHE STEPPED INSIDE, UNAVOIDABLY announced. The door swung shut behind her, a soft hiccup from the hinge as it clicked into place and the bell faded into silence. She rubbed her neck, the beads of sweat already dry to her touch, and then shoved her hands hard into her pockets. She wouldn't. She couldn't. *Not again.*

The man at the register, just a boy really, kept his head down, counting something and bouncing on his heels. Music. Ear buds in, good. He was new, even better. Not that it mattered, not that he noticed her. But a new person was better. Fewer memories. She slid toward the rows of books before he could glance up. They'd get to know each other soon—no. Eyes closed, standing next to the stationary, she took a slow breath. It was too much; it was a mistake to come. She looked in her pocketbook, fumbled with a pack of gum until she thought she could continue. Zipping her bag shut she darted towards the back. Far from the man. Far from the wide windows and the busy sidewalk. Far from the eyes. Her shoulder dinged the corner of a display and she stumbled, caught herself, stumbled again. She glanced at the tracker on her wrist, more comfortable with a blinking digital heart and a climbing number than the signals coming from her own body. *Not again.* A glance at the shelves, nothing fell. Not a page out of place. Cashier Boy hummed faintly. She didn't try to figure out the tune, didn't want to focus on him. Another step closer to the back corner. She felt dizzy.

The classics section was a reprieve, a moment of absolute clarity, no desire, nothing clouding her judgement. Old smells. Older pages. Still, she reached out to touch the spine of *Frankenstein*, a Modern Library edition by the looks of its rough red cover and diminutive size. Shelley was a friend. Delicious. The pad of her finger smoothed the spine and she shivered. It was coming now, the dread gathering to billow around her. Nausea crept into her stomach and made her breath hitch. It was coming. Her fingernail snagged on the cover and tore away. Just the edge, really. Just enough to rip and bleed, add a deeper spot of red to the faded spine.

She stuffed her hand back in her pocket and ran her thumb in circles over the new edge of her nail like a mantra, *ignore it ignore it ignore it* until she couldn't, and then she shoved her finger in her mouth and sucked, hard. Her knuckle crushed her lip, made it bruise and swell. A sharp inhale through her nose, a few steps and she would be there. So close. She forced herself to stop. Let the anticipation build until she started to wobble, spots dancing in front of her eyes. *Wait.*

"Are you okay?" Cashier Boy flipped the hair back from his forehead, the faintest outline of a mustache attempting to mount his lip.

"Yes." It's more gargle than word, her finger still halfway down her throat and she can tell he's not going to walk away. She wouldn't have. She sounded like a garbage disposal trying to speak. She took out the now sopping wet finger and waved it in the general direction of her head.

"Migraine."

He nodded, tapped his ear and tinny music filled the space between them as he turned. She watched him walk away, humming again. Her right hand stayed out of her mouth but her left hand, hidden deep in her pocket, pinched the tiniest piece of flesh she could grasp. Pinched it until it screamed.

"Yes," she whispered, and turned to the corner. One more step.

She stood exactly center between the shelves and then sank to her knees. Her place. Her books. It was almost impossible to find the right kind back when it started. She'd tried clubs and subscriptions and all of the usual things. Until she realized she wasn't a usual thing. But here, there were choices, used or new, bent or brittle. Here, she could forage, and hunt, find the right book find the right voice. The right flavor. She closed her eyes and reached out sliding an unseen volume off the shelf. Horror, of course. Always horror. Monsters beget monsters beget monsters. The serpent doesn't eat her tail, she makes more serpents. And those, she eats.

She didn't bother with the cover or opening her eyes. She flipped past it, past the author's page and all the copyright nonsense to the words, the words. They drifted off the paper as she inhaled. Her fingertip and thumb hovered and then grasped the top right corner of a page. She tore it ever so slowly, ever so cleanly, ever so silently from the binding. The words were there, all there, waiting for her as her breath came faster, and when she couldn't wait, couldn't possibly wait any longer she crumpled it and shoved the entire page into her mouth past the point of gagging all the way down her throat, and then slid her empty hand back out. Rested it on her teeth. Felt the ink slick on her tongue and let her fingers play with her lips, tracing them in black. Reached for the book again. Another page. Sometimes chewing. Sometimes not. Teeth and tongue black. Again. She licked her fingers and sucked the images inside her. Eyes closed. Head back. Again. Again. Again. Until every page was torn out, until her cheeks were smeared with words and black saliva dripped down her chin like spilled ink.

WHEN HORSES CRY

---

a true story

ART, HISTORY, AND ABSOLUTELY NO AIRPLANES. IT WAS A short list, but critical to vacationing with a six-month-old. On a thick day in July, we boarded a train north to Savannah. I watched the landscape slide by— trees, sun, a section of fence. I drifted to sleep, daughter in my arms, when the palms were still stabbing the sky. I woke hours later with my cheek stuck to old vinyl and my husband gently taking the baby.

"We're here."

There was nothing to be seen. Flat land and a maximum building height of four floors gave Savannah a low profile. But she was waiting like all old cities, if crouched a bit lower than the others. Closer to what lay beneath the ground, closer to the past. Not a palm to be found on the drive to our hotel but plenty of twisted oaks and dead moss hanging. It seemed impossible that the trees were alive under all that moss; it seemed impossible that the moss was alive under all that moss. What might have been a vibrant green back home was silver gray, a clouded canopy overhead and afternoon made nightfall. Our hotel made up for it with a bright garden between the walk and the front door.

The concierge was chipper enough as we checked in, but I sank onto the lobby couch, still drowsy from the ride and the six months of sleep deprivation only an infant can provide. My daughter took it all in as we flipped the pages of the binder waiting on the coffee table. I am incapable of not reading, if there is reading to be had. Menus and coupons gave way to the good stuff, the history of the hotel. The past for every building in Savannah, I soon learned, was a summary of the deaths that took place within its walls and on its lawns. Example: Room 207 must not be let out to guests because of the screaming of the horses as they burned. It seems that Room 207 sat above what had once been the stable. And the stable caught fire during the night, as all truly dramatic fires do, trapping the horses and burning them alive. It being nearly impossible to remove a scared horse from their stable, their safe place, I imagined hooves pounding the earth as the fire crawled up the walls, their terrified eyes reflecting the smoke, and then the flames, and then the blackness. The screams, it seems, still echo.

Room key in hand, we waited for the elevator to the second floor because there is no climbing the stairs with a baby and a baby's paraphernalia. The concierge had a last word of advice. I was expecting restaurant hours or a check out time, but it was simply this: "Don't mind the grandfather clock in the lobby if you happen to hear it chiming midnight, it hasn't worked for years." It was a quiet ride to the second floor. Our room was nowhere near Room 207 and the former stables, but I put something colorful on the television. For the baby. For myself. I let the high-pitched voices and swirling shapes soothe as I remade our room into a home for three. There is no vacation with a baby, after all. She babbled. I puttered.

Vacation or no, the room was sorted, and we made plans to explore. I wondered if the whole town was going to gas light us or if it was just part of that little hotel's marketing – scares for the tourists, no extra charge. The charm was free and plentiful, every garden held back by a wrought iron gate, every square lorded over by a statue, every statue blessed by a church. And the trees. Always the trees, blurred edges and twisted roots. We visited a modern museum just to remember that walls could be vertical and free of vegetation, and so our daughter could test her young lungs and gain us an escort to the exit. There was one terrifying moment when we found ourselves in a café filled with elderly women bedecked in a swarm of red and purple and the word cult crossed my mind as we quickly ran off to find yet another green common, another bench. I wondered if we would see the sun again, or if we would simply bake, and melt, and slide off the bench onto the grass under the trees. We learned proper names: Southern Live Oaks weeping Spanish Moss. It seemed important to identify them as *live* oaks, as everything else was clearly dead, or nearly dead, or caught somewhere in between.

I was drunk on gardens and people watching, but my husband wanted to honor the ghostly side of Savannah, and the city agreed that was best. A bookstore gave us, "Hi, welcome, ghost stories are on aisle two. Oh, and stay away from the back eastern corner now that the sun has set, all right?" A historic home offered, "Thanks for stopping in y'all. You're welcome to roam everywhere except the basement, the door'll shut on its own and won't open unlocked or not." It seemed possible to embrace it, even for me. If the locals were so friendly, so matter of fact about it all, then maybe I could handle a ghost tour. I don't call myself a believer, nor do I think that I'm particularly afraid of ghosts. More like appropriately respectful and not willing to antagonize. But this felt closer to an inside joke, a family story that takes on legendary status, no campfire boogeymen, no hooks scratching on windows. Just good food and friendly people. And that I did believe in— good food and friendly people, gardens in front of dollhouse colored houses, sweet tea, and old gravestones. I told myself the dead must be happy, to have so much attention. That it would be disrespectful not to go on a ghost tour in this, the most haunted city in America. And then there was the baby. I'd have the baby with me and could always beg out if it felt... if it felt wrong. I simply wouldn't listen if the horses screamed.

Waiting for a tour to start with a six-month-old is an excellent way to determine who likes kids. She was asleep so I ran the judgment gauntlet and headed to the back of the trolley when they finally let us board. Our guide was quite matter of fact, no goofy spooky voices or dripping fangs in spite of the ghost tour placards plastering the sides of the trolley announcing our intentions and the number to book a tour. Perhaps the dead don't read. Perhaps the dead don't care if we use them. He filled us in on his city. On her long, war-filled history, the piracy and the privateering. The Riverfront. The seaside. I'd forgotten we were on the coast in spite of the seafood-packed menus and the smell. Cicadas and mosquitos slowly let go of twilight, the air was still, and I was reluctant to draw deep, to allow myself to taste the night air. We hadn't been out late, unwilling to test the hospitality of the nearest bar with a crying child. Unwilling as well to test the local mix of champagne, rum, brandy, and bourbon on my breast milk. But this, this evening air was its own cocktail sharing the sea and the swamp with the flowers, the scent of death salted and mulched a thousand times over, bodies buried and forgotten and found. I was suddenly aware of gardens grown from soil well-fed for centuries, and it felt good to remember that life comes from death and not simply the other way around. I smiled, and it startled me to realize I'd been holding my breath since we got on board.

We began and ended with death. Death on every corner in every possible way: poisons and duels and piracy and plague, the last was most pedestrian but left a high body count. No count at all of the bodies that lay beneath the colonists' boots, or the generations lost between then and now. A simple pause of the trolley at a street corner narrowed the death toll to that block, recorded and recited by heart, and that was before we arrived at the cemetery. It was well after dark when we heard of the civil war soldiers, desperate for warmth, who cracked open the tombs of their revolutionary brothers and crept inside to wait out the night. An above ground walk seemed manageable and considerably less rude, so I whispered a prayer and an apology and stayed firmly on the path. I chose not to peer into the mausoleum, unwilling to wake whatever slumbered there. But the others did, eyeballs reaching into shadows, hoping for a glimpse of what remained. We were last to reboard, rushing felt too disrespectful. Maybe they watched us walk away. Maybe they wondered why we were so eager to leave. Maybe they slept and didn't care.

We weren't the only ones grown quiet as we headed to the finale. Even the guide simply told us we had one more stop and let us alone with our thoughts. I was proud of myself; I'd made it this far. Surely I could handle what came next? Walking and listening were easy, and the term haunted house felt, well, it felt overdone. There were simply too many of us, a group this big wasn't going to experience anything unusual. I'd squinted my way through enough movies to know that. We pulled up in front of another beautiful three-story structure. Shuttered windows. Wrap around porch. The house was simple if huge, and painted pink or maybe peach, with a few smaller buildings scattered around— old stables converted to a garage, new life for old ways. Ivy climbed the walls, playing hide and seek with the roofline. It massed and reached the top at only one end, the other untouched and smooth as if the house wore a deep green dressing gown and decided to show us some shoulder. It was every house we'd seen that day, and like no haunted house ever depicted. Not a speck of dust, not a cobweb in sight, though I'm told spiders, insects, even scorpions nest in the relentless moss. It was lovely and quiet and made me imagine living behind those windows. I suspect they started us in the basement so that it wouldn't feel like we were there for an open house.

We stood in a low-ceilinged room, close together in the dark. I could barely see my daughter's face inches from my own, but I felt her warm and safe. The guide dropped his voice lower still as we learned of deadly crimes that took place nearby, blood soaking through the soil, blood whispering pain and passion and death, layers of blood sinking to the water that seeped beneath us and bursting through new tales told over years. It was horrific to be sure, humans killing each other is never pleasant, and I felt my breath begin to catch, the air growing still in my lungs as past pain disturbed and delighted the room, the other occupants only shadows around me and I wondered if our numbers had grown, if we might have someone else in our group, someone not willing to let us visit in peace, someone who might feel angry at our entertainment. The guide paused in his litany and asked us to listen close, to see if we could sense anything in the silence. It was quiet and close and I shut my eyes to see if I could tell the difference between open and not, between the light and the dark, when a deep unmistakable sigh split the air between us. I twitched; the others gasped and broke apart and I decided to let them think the worst as my daughter stretched in her sleep and swallowed the sigh that scared us all. I suppose some of us forgot she was there.

The tour moved slowly to the upper levels, where we learned of a young servant, though let's be honest, she was enslaved, no one jumps to their death if they have options. We walked through the courtyard she couldn't escape and looked up to a third story window. It was tall, and rounded at the top, and when we made our way upstairs and saw it at the end of a terribly long hallway, a narrow runway spanning the breadth of the house, it seemed designed for suicide. The guide bestowed his penultimate gift – we would each be given a moment to see the full length of her path, a moment to contemplate the last forty feet of her life, the final stretch of a run that ended with her body hurtling through the window and falling to the cobblestones below. One moment of freedom in a lifetime before gravity snatched her back and slammed her to the ground. It was a spot she came back to regularly, he assured us, and I wondered if she visited the window or her freedom. I hoped it was the latter and not her death, but my heart told me she was trapped in the house she longed to escape. Fate married to irony. It was horrifying, her circumstances were horrifying, but I wasn't afraid of her. I was afraid for her. I felt my stomach clench, that a life of could come to this, and yet she was the scary one because she was trapped here, trapped where no one helped and suddenly I was glad— maybe she did scare people, maybe she did appear and drift and chill their bones. Maybe it helped. Clearly I was not the right person for the tour which shouldn't have surprised me. I was the child who cried over the horses in westerns, and not just when they got shot and lay twisted and bleeding. I cried if they had barbed wire cutting into them from a brush with a fence. It just didn't seem fair that they were hurt because of the stupid humans on their backs and my annoyance continued even after I learned it was faked for the camera.

Enough distracting myself. I held my breath as we crossed the landing and quickly turned my head to gaze toward the window. The hall was green from the dark wood floors to the ceiling high above us and it seemed to me that the ivy made its way inside after all. The window stood far away, as if the house was stretching itself and there was a tiny step stool of polished dark wood at its base. Odd. Why have a step stool near a window, a window that nearly reaches the floor? I saw —no, I imagined her bare foot landing on that stool before launching herself away into the night, away from her sorrow and pain in a shatter of glass and wood and I held my breath. I wasn't given a glimpse of her, not even a shadow of her white nightgown. I don't think anyone was, though a few people sucked in their breath as we passed. I didn't really expect to see her, but I whispered, "I hope you're okay" just in case she was nearby, then took the few short steps into the room that would wrap the tour.

It was a beautiful room or would have been, but the stately furniture was pushed back to the walls to make space for us. I could see now that it was deep green wallpaper; it flowed in from the hallway and upward to high ceilings that ended in darkness, crown moldings just visible in the shadows. There really is no substitute for old architecture. Our guide was delighted to share that this very room, This Very Room, was once featured on a ghost hunter show. I was exhausted from my own mental gymnastics, but I appreciated him making us feel like we got our money's worth. And what's this, the experts had readings and measurements that were considered "very intense"? I failed to see how a mechanical instrument could record these things, but I was determined to play along. The dead were not simply felt, proof was needed and the team captured something in an audio recording no less. Would we like to listen?

We would, to no one's surprise.

Lights off and silence. Static. Then a woman's voice, keening, screaming for her life, for mercy, throat splitting cries oh god help me, god help me and I thought enough, enough already. This is crystal clear; do they not know how obvious it is that this was done in a sound studio? Well done, I'll give them that, but please. I work with actors. I know performances and this was a bit too perfect. She was in so much pain. Absolutely brutal. And I was mad, not just that they laid it on so thick, but that this pain was for our amusement. Real audio or not, someone died here and who were we to be entertained by that?

My husband was quietly listening at my side, everyone in fact, was listening politely, intently, so I thought, fine, we're all playing along. I get it, I'll just stand here, it's a haunted house thing. But then it got worse. Begging. A voice begging please begging stop. I was nothing but the sound of her voice. It was clear she was being beaten, she was being hurt, and why wasn't anyone helping her? Even as I listened, I felt my heart pound and I touched my daughter's skin to prove the voice wasn't real, she's warm and she's close and the voice is not real. I closed my eyes but that made the woman easier to see, so I opened them and stared down at where the floor should be, tucked my daughter under my chin, and swayed just a little as she somehow slept through it. And finally, finally it was over, the voice, the cry broke past words into a long sob, and then white noise, and then nothing.

There was a murmur in the room as we began to file out, and I wondered if anyone else was considering the work of a recording like that. I focused on the practicalities of sound editing, proud that I hadn't been fooled by the tape. Maybe there was no woman. Maybe it was all for show.

"That was a little much, don't you think?" I asked my husband, still cradling the baby in my arms and trying to laugh it off. "That woman?" His face was blank, so I tried again, "On the tape, all that screaming, it seemed a little over-produced, right?"

"All I heard was static," he said.

MOO

Transcription:
FOY51AA
Farming Sector
Unknown

"Racism ended the day the aliens appeared. We were all fighting so hard, fighting to end it, fighting to deny it, fighting to help it endure, fighting to prove it existed. None of us saw the end coming, the deus ex machina that would reach out and crush us in its grip. Sure, people tried to keep it going, tried to keep sexism going too, but the aliens, with no sense of sight and no distinction of gender—who knew how they procreated, someone said they thought themselves into being? Anyway, they certainly weren't bothering to make distinctions among us, except in terms of taste and flavor. And there were no other distinctions, didn't matter if you were ten or a hundred and five, an Olympic athlete or a desk jockey, a chef or a sex worker— there was just already eaten by the aliens and waiting to be eaten by the aliens. Simple.

And so, the farms began. They roughly classified all the mammals together, so droves of us died when they tossed us in the ocean with the dolphins. Made for rather smelly beaches for a while. But then they realized that we were the least intelligent among the mammals, and the most likely to force the planet into expiration, so they began to single us out as a species for extinction. It made sense. They were beings that were intent on getting every last juicy drop out of every planet they invaded, after all "waste not want not" was the official motto engraved on their ships when we finally learned to decipher the code. That's a lie, we didn't decipher their code, they figured out a way to write it so anyone could read it. Even people who couldn't read. So yeah. Superior. Our claim to number one was the top of the list of species to eat, invasive and frankly proliferating as we were. They called us "Virri" which is just virus we later figured out. We said we were an apex predator, we never said we were clever. Or maybe it's just that they treated us that way, treated us like something to be eradicated that we gave ourselves the nick-name. I can't remember exactly how it all went down. Just that one minute we were all in trying to kill each other while we took selfies, and the next minute all the technology was gone. Like all of it. Instantly. And we just stood there, frozen.

People called them settlements because it sounds nicer but they were farms. It wasn't all bad, until the reapings of course. No yelling and screaming, not like in the movies that got it almost but not quite right. Reapings were quiet. Very quiet. You were there, and then you were gone, and the only reason we knew it was a reaping was because it happened in clusters.

What else? Oh, we went bad if we were isolated from one another, so families were together. But we were free to wander. It just made more sense, you know, the way chickens are happier if they get to roam around and eat bugs? Free range humans. They did keep a close watch on violence. And we were fed. And disease didn't seem to bother anyone, at least, once they insisted that we take care of each other in that really gentle 'people who don't take care of each other get eaten' way. It was like living with a super sweet kinder-garten teacher who finds your flesh delicious, so behave. People were generally healthy and generally nice. Anyone remotely associated with violence didn't just disappear, they exploded. I don't know how they did it, it's not like we ever saw any weapons. Someone said that they put something in our food, but I don't know. It didn't make sense. I saw it happen a bunch of times but up close only once.

It was in the beginning, when they were still figuring us out. There were experiments. Nothing too weird actually, at least not that I heard about. Everyone who thought the arrival of the aliens was going to mean bizarro intergalactic sex was seriously disappointed. Seems that intelligence is sexy so we never stood a chance. It was embarrassing frankly, the low opinion of our collective intellect "out there." I was in a group that did the "dog test." They'd show us dogs of all different kinds, to see if we knew they were dogs, even if they didn't look exactly the same. They just don't make those kinds of distinctions, it was all really mammals/not mammals, so the racism thing was impossible for them to comprehend, parsing an entire species by skin color baffled them, and they understandably assumed we might not be bright. It was like – here's a dog with short hair, here's a dog with long hair, are they both dogs?

Oh, yeah, people failed. Spectacularly. Some of them were suicides, I'm sure, even before the projections. And some people are just deep in the bones racist, just could not process not only their own equality with the rest of us, but their undeniable inferiority to our ah, visitors. Distinctions of superiority for every mother loving thing. I was in a group with a guy tatted up to the eyeballs, literally, with shit I'd never seen except in movies and history books, and even then it was on flags not inked onto a body, and we knew exactly what kind of hater he was because it was spelled out right there on his forehead. It was mesmerizing in a wow, humans are stupid kind of way. Anyhow, we're all sitting there, going "dog, dog, dog, elephant, dog" because it wasn't hard to figure out that's what they wanted, that was the point of the whole exercise, to see if we could recognize species. Must have been an early test, I'd hope most of us know the difference between a dog and an elephant. Anyway, this idiot with the ink starts going off about how this or that dog is special and a more important breed and all this other stuff. They gave him like three chances and it was just this compulsive bullshit inability for him to say that is a fucking dog. I don't know. Maybe it was pent up nonsense because he'd been unable to spout about humans since they arrived, so he transferred it to canines? Maybe he was tired of living where all human lives were equal, and equal to the cows for that matter? Rats too I guess, when it comes down to it, a mammal is a mammal.

Anyway, got himself good and worked up. I watched his neck flush and a vein start to bulge and stepped away – the evaporating wasn't always exactly precise from what I'd seen, and I wasn't ready to exit the planet because this idiot had to claim supremacy. So, genius gets his good old rage going and goes after one of the dogs they'd lined up in front of us. Lunges for it across the room, laid out horizontal, hands reaching for the dog's neck. The dog, a bored looking pitty, turned his head just in time to see this guy hit the floor and start to twitch, the immediate pre-cursor to the invisibility show. I'd seen it a hundred times already but I did watch long enough to see the dog lift his leg and take a whiz. I wondered if they slowed the process on purpose when the piss splashed in his open screaming mouth, but maybe not, because he exploded and then evaporated before the arc finished, so the puddle of urine on the floor was all that was left. He was a pretty big dude. Hope they were hungry. Somebody else said they didn't eat the ones who insisted on being racist, but I've never seen anybody ask a cow if he got along with his neighbors before they slaughtered him, so I can't imagine why they'd care.

After a while, people just stopped being violent, no matter what the cause. Or maybe all the violent people died? I mean, seeing a guy explode when he tries to rape someone, well, it tends to turn people off to that kind of thing. And then of course there was the wave of "alien lover" comments directed at women who weren't unhappy that they no longer had to worry about assault. It's a heady thing to have a weight taken away that's been there since the start of time, and understandably there was more than one woman feeling grateful about living with the same freedom and power as a man for the rest of her life. However short that might be. And nobody seemed to give a shit about people's orientation either, all that stuff – it was like suddenly nobody had time to get into each other's business because everyone recognized – there's eaten by the aliens, and there's not eaten by the aliens. Yet.

There was a lot of singing, probably because a bunch of the tech music stuff disappeared in the beginning and people were desperate to share something they both knew. And then people started using instruments more, guitars and drums at first, then violins and flutes popping up, ever so politely bartered for, you know. No one wanted to evaporate because of a plastic recorder. So yeah, it was a lot like, well, I guess like in the olden days. People grew food, sometimes just to have something to do and sometimes because, well, to have something to do. People started singing all the time, which was fine when they could sing but man, when they couldn't.

You don't realize what auto tune is doing for the world until it's gone.

Rich and poor? Nah, those distinctions left pretty fast. Well, the rich were eaten quickly, these alien types they like a healthy food source. There were sections of the planet that were going to take a while to get up to speed, I guess. As you can imagine, North America, Europe, all the "developed" countries got nibbled at first, and then when they were done with the first wave, or first course maybe, they left us to ourselves and only took what they needed. And with no need for money, other things became precious. It's weird to operate in a world that can't be violent. A lot of people seemed really annoyed by it, tried to hold onto their prejudices, but that just got them a one-way trip to the big ship. At first, it wasn't much of a deterrent, but then they started projecting what was happening, or had happened, directly into our brains and folks straightened up fast. People might be willing to deny what they see but when you feel your own flesh being peeled like a grape, it doesn't even matter if it's real, when you wake up from that, you think, maybe skin color doesn't matter so much.

And then it got to be like the real olden days, you know, when they'd talk about the gods interfering and all that. People started praying for good harvests which seemed a little pointless since we were the harvest, but everyone just figured it couldn't hurt. It's odd, to be praying to gods when you don't need anything except to be rescued from what some people thought were, well, gods. It's tricky because we never saw them. We just knew it was a them because they told us, "We are who we are." Honestly, it was like being invaded by a bunch of suburban yoga moms who have too much time on their hands and spend their days propping up each other's wine habits posting pithy 'go get 'em girl' sayings that would be better left on a cross-stitched pillow in your Granny's attic.

Other than that, things were pretty normal. Except - no kids born. These guys were all about population control, and of course, once they went through us, they could start on the other mammals. But they were really careful with the food supply, I don't know how many planets they've already gone through, but they're not gorging themselves. It's more like that grazing diet that people used to talk about? That eat several small meals a day thing? I guess that's what having a big brain does. Oh, they kept us separate from the carnivores for a while, once they finally got us classified. Apparently, our lack of significant teeth and claws excited them, we were the apex predator, right, must have something up our sleeves. Mostly they wanted to see how we'd do unarmed against a bear. Not well. Not well at all.

I almost forgot – the sex is great. No risk of getting pregnant, so women didn't have to listen to anyone bitch and moan about what we did or didn't do with our collective uteri. And it was a given that anyone having sex was only doing it for pleasure, no kids and no rape after all, so yeah. That part's pretty sweet. United against a common enemy and all that, I guess. It's a bummer that we never know when we're going to go, but all in all, people are taking care of each other now. Not sure if it matters, not sure if any of it matters, but people got to thinking if these guys don't like violence, maybe, just maybe taking care of each other is a way to escape, you know *poof.* So sure, some people are still in steady relationships, but honestly, divorce is way, way, way down and so is marriage for that matter. Something about not knowing when you're gonna go makes people want to work things out. And it's not like they let us argue about who gets a piece of paper that says they get to be together anymore.

Um, total lack of conflict seems like. Which reminds me!

The story tellers – oh yeah, the storytellers – they get a lot of attention. It's okay to tell stories, it's okay to get people excited. Apparently, they've finally proven, somewhere in the galaxy, that a book or music can't make a non-violent person violent. That, and probably because there's no alcohol or drugs anymore. Nope. No addiction to anything anymore. They don't want it ruining the livestock is what it comes down to. So I can only assume they like our livers. Sure, it's a little weird, having that stuff taken away. For a while, it was a great way to go, because getting out of control was a sure-fire way to disappear and people did it, you know, to escape, to end it all. But then the rumors started that when people disappeared, they didn't die right away, that they were eaten while they were still fresh, and fresh meant alive, so suddenly it didn't seem like a great way to go. And then they started the projections which pretty much confirmed it and everyone chilled out really damn quick. And then of course, a lot of the addictions led to violence of different kinds, and that was a definite way to go, so in the beginning there was a lot of... a lot of reapings. And no way to know if some new rule would be discovered. Some new way to get yourself blown up.

Now? Like today? We just kind of go about our business, and hope our loved ones aren't next, but if they are, well at least they know we love them. It's not like we have any choice.

They used to say live every day like it's your last, but as a species? Yeah, we didn't really get that until it was."

CUL DE SAC

TERRI, THREE HOURS AGO

Terri was in her garage at sunrise. She sat in one corner and the box sat in another, diagonally across from her. "Round three," she thought, and then, "I'm ready for you, you little fuckers."

She had her feet planted and her hands on her knees, tools in a jumble around her feet: a hammer, a broom, the leaf blower. Her arms were raw to the elbows after three rounds of scrubbing with a baking soda paste and a bamboo fiber washcloth. Ready. Here in the garage where she could deal with it properly. Privately. Where she could address her many concerns. Where she could finish this. The door was open just in case she had to haul it back outside, and the bright, clear sky meant the garage was already slashed in half by the sun. She sat in the shadow. The box sat in the light, where she could keep an eye on it.

BRENDA, THREE NIGHTS AGO

Chicken. No—pasta. No—chicken. It was the same conversation she'd had with herself every afternoon between four o'clock and dinner time so she wasn't really listening. At least Amelia was quiet. Upstairs, occupied with whatever came in the box from the play group. She'd been relieved to see it on the front step that morning, delivered by On Time Terri. Terri who was ever so organized, from her hair to her feet. Brenda was willing to bet the inside of her car was clean, even under the car seat. Terri who likely had a monthly meal plan. Monthly. Yearly. Brenda was certain Terri never discussed and simultaneously ignored conversations with herself about what to have for dinner.

Pasta. Chicken. No—pasta. Wait, it was pasta last night, wasn't it? She couldn't remember. What no one tells you, what no one warns you of, is the mind-numbing sameness of the days. That's what led to the obsession with kids, she was certain. The only thing that changed in these houses were the kids. Probably why the play group was a near constant dissection of achievements large and small. And that included bowel movements. She nearly laughed. Her husband had suggested photographing Amelia's ridiculous bowel movements. So impressive. Well. At least they were laughing then. It was better than whatever this was, this post fight, post Fight silence that settled over them. Scratch that. It wasn't silence, silence you could feel. This was apathy. Apathy that might quickly change to anger if she wasn't quicker about dinner.

She had to make a decision. Chicken. No pasta. She was about to give up and dial for pizza when she heard a creak and a thump overhead. "Amelia? Meels?" No sound. No crying either, but still. She climbed the stairs, running her hand along the smooth bannister. She'd always wanted a banister. It was the only thing on her wish list when they bought the house. A banister she could decorate. Something he liked to remind her of when the 'stuff' piled up on the bottom step. You wanted the second story Muffin so you could decorate the stairs, remember? She remembered. She remembered when Muffin didn't conjure up her waistline. She climbed to the second floor and walked to the bonus room. It was supposed to be her office, when Amelia went to school and she went back to work. It was supposed to be an art room, before Amelia was born. It was supposed to be a guest room, back when they thought of course everyone would want to visit their house, in the almost but not quite new subdivision. It was supposed to be a lot of things. Amelia was fine, but she caught her climbing on top of the box and jumping off.

"What are you doing honey?" She tried not to panic, the way the other mothers did. Kids climbed stuff. She did when she was a kid. Trees. Ladders. Pyramids of other kids.

Amelia turned at the top and jumped off again, hands over her head, concentrating. It was her expression that startled Brenda – it didn't match the action. There was no laugh. No cry of joy, no cry of despair, just quiet concentration. She asked again.

"What are you doing honey?"

"Flyin." Of course. What else would it be?

"Looks like fun." Even though it didn't. Even though the line of her child's brow seemed more grimace than grin. Amelia turned and climbed on top of the box again. Brenda noticed nothing had been taken out of it.

"So what was in there anyway?" Jump. Turn. Climb. Jump.

"Flying."

"In the box honey. What was in the box honey?" Amelia landed, grabbed a car and flung it at Brenda's head. It missed her face and smashed into the wall behind her. Chipped the paint. The kid proof paint. The car was indestructible, so it slid down the wall behind the bookcase to gather dust.

"I'm. Flying."

Brenda put her hands up. "All right all right pilot, just be careful, please?"

Amelia ignored her and went back to jumping. Brenda heard the scramble to the top of the box and the thump as she landed. And by the time she got to the first floor again, just the thump. The kitchen was as she left it. She opened the cupboard to pull out a box of pasta and was met with her lack of shopping. *Thump*. Fine. Chicken it is. She pulled the bird from its wrappings over the sink, let the juice drip into the disposal and tried not to look at the skin, wet and dimpled, holes that used to hold feathers.

She grabbed a knife from the stand and heard "What's this hack job?" clear as day. Clear as night she guessed was more accurate, night when he said it, looking at a shredded sirloin in front of him. "Why don't you try sharpening the knives occasionally?" Fair enough. *Thump*. She took out the silver sharpener and braced it against the counter, running the blade down the edge. It scraped in a deeply satisfying way. And then *thump* from overhead. Scrape. *Thump*. Scrape. *Thump*. It was beautiful, really, when you thought about it. When you gave in and let it rest in your ear. Scrape. *Thump*. Like the world's shortest song. Two notes. Scrape. *Thump*. Scrape. *Thump*. It was getting softer or maybe her hands were getting slower.

Scrape.

Thump.

Scrape.

Scrape.

Scrape.

. . .

"WHAT THE HELL! AMELIA NO!"

Brenda stepped out of the kitchen just as Emmett slammed into her shoulder, spinning her around but not far enough, not far enough to miss Amelia's body, climbing over the rail, her foot leaving the box she'd shoved up against it swinging over, over the rail and pushing off, pushing up, into the air of the foyer Brenda twisted her neck up to see the height of her arc before she dropped out of sight. Out of sight because she couldn't take her eyes off the place where she had been, the space now, where she wasn't. She thought about the light fixture up there, how much she hated it, she thought about the ceiling, it must have been so hard to paint, two floors up in the open space, this weird open space that served no purpose but as an area to gaze up, at the railing, at the second floor and that gorgeous bannister winding its way down to the floor.

The floor. She wouldn't look at the floor, her eyes were closed now, wouldn't look at what might be on the floor. Until she heard footsteps, running up the stairs, light and fast and she opened her eyes to see the blur of Amelia's denims streak by on the landing, run into her room and slam the door. Heard the grunt from the floor that was Emmett, climbing back to his feet.

"You caught her," she whispered.

Emmett didn't answer, didn't look at Brenda, just climbed the stairs after Amelia, pausing at the box.

"What the hell is this?"

"It's a box. It's just a box of toys."

He ignored her and went to Amelia's room. She could hear her girl crying from where she was. Still standing in the doorway, willing her mind to stop playing *what if what if what if what if*. She dropped the sharpener onto the nearest counter and ran up the stairs, but Emmett was already there, of course. Of course.

"Hey buddy what's going on?" as he scooped up their child and gave her a squeeze. "That was something Meels. Did you bump your head?" Amelia shook it vigorously to dispel that myth and squirmed to be put down. She wiped her snot on her sleeve and looked past Emmett at the box.

"I'm going to take that downstairs now and why don't you wash up for dinner?" Amelia stepped into the bathroom her room shared with the bonus room. The bonus room, that was supposed to be a nursery, when they had another child. Or an art room or an office or a guest room or. Or nothing. Emmett glanced at Brenda, just long enough to turn a shared look into an accusation before taking the box downstairs. He grunted as he did.

"How did you get this thing up here? And how did she drag it down the hall?"

Brenda didn't answer. She was standing on the landing, looking over the railing at the floor of the foyer. At the marble table with a sharp corner. At the rug, crumpled to the side where Emmett slid on it. She wondered if he'd catch her if she jumped.

"She jumps off stuff now? She jumps off this?" Emmett was back on the landing, his voice somehow soft and sharp at the same time.

"Almost like a child."

It was the wrong thing to say, she knew it was the wrong thing to say, it leapt from her mouth with the carelessness of a child, the terrifying carelessness of a child, but she couldn't claim it. Couldn't own it, because if she did, if she took responsibility for that climb, for that leap that would mean it happened. That the space she watched for so long from below, the empty space, could have been everything she had left.

"Yeah, a child who gets hurt."

Brenda spun on the spot and headed back downstairs,

trying to outpace the accusations that had to follow, it was her fault, it was and no argument and no apology would change that so why not leave her be?

"What were you doing? Not making dinner I guess," as he followed her into the kitchen. "Where'd that box come from anyway?"

"It's a toy box."

"You went shopping?"

"No, it's the shared toy box. The play group one. We rotate, remember."

"I don't remember all those flowers and shit."

"Yeah, well, I don't make the boxes."

"You just let her jump off them. Whatever. I'm gonna change. Let me know when it's ready."

She heard him open the drawer behind her and grab the corkscrew as he slid a bottle from the wine rack. The cupboard door opened a moment later and she could picture him pulling the decanter off the shelf. Wine has to breath after all. Make sure it breathes. He was out of the room when she whispered, "Nice to see you too." She preheated the oven and picked up the sharpener again.

Scrape.

And from the other room, *thump*.

Brenda came to herself with knife in hand, standing over the sink with the water running. She thought it was water. It felt like water, running down her hands. But when she reached to turn the faucet off, her skin was red, her hand transformed into something else. Glistening. Alien. Blood dripped off her fingers. Drops hit the sink and stayed, this one palest pink and this one crimson, thick. Both hands were covered. She quickly placed the knife in the sink and rinsed them, looking for an injury. Nothing. Not even a nick. She was fine. She turned to the table and slipped, landing on her ass on the linoleum. A black mass pooled off the corner of the table and her legs were sticky with it. What the hell. She pulled herself up and the vomit rose in her throat. The table was covered. Blood coated the remains of a dinner. She could see Amelia's little train tray, mashed potatoes smeared around but not eaten, her booster seat strapped into the chair. Where was she? Where was Emmett? Her stomach twisted and she turned in time to puke into the sink then ran for the stairs, ran all the way to Amelia's room, burst in, and there she was, asleep. Pudgy fist tucked under her chin, like she was in the middle of listening to a story. She stepped toward the bed and smacked her shin on the corner of the box. Amelia must have dragged it there; Brenda could see the marks in the rug. She sat on the edge of the bed, rubbed her own shin with one hand and stroked Amelia's forehead with the other. One breath. Another. She was fine. She was breathing, she was even in pajamas. How did she do that... Emmett. She peeked out the window, his car was still in the driveway.

"Em?" She called down the hallway. "Honey?" as she came around the corner of their door. Nothing. He wasn't lying on the bed; the TV was off. The bedclothes weren't even wrinkled. She checked Amelia again before walking back downstairs to the nightmare on the table. Wait. Wait. Was it blood? Was it? It looked like wine. The remains of the broken decanter bottle lay on its side near Emmett's seat, and the bottle itself was knocked over. It wasn't the first time wine had soaked the table. Particularly if you aren't paying attention and you have an active three-year old. Particularly if there's an argument going on. So much wine though. So much. The dishes had pieces of chicken scattered among them, the flesh shiny and pink. Undercooked. Undercooked poultry. He must be livid with her. She couldn't remember the fight though. She picked up the dishes and scraped them into the disposal, listening to the whirl of the motor and a crunch that should not have been there. A bone. A bone and undercooked honestly, it must have been one hell of a fight. She started to scrape another plate. A hunk of meat stuck in the fork and she held it, eye level. Completely raw. She dropped it in the disposal and turned it on. There was that crunch again. She turned it off and ran the water, pulled the rubber seal from the sink drain and peered into the hole. A glint in the corner. She poked it with a fork, head resting on the counter, trying to get a good look. It wasn't stuck, but she couldn't grab at it. She took a breath and pushed up her sleeve. Thought about putting her hand all the way into the disposal, then thought about the blades somehow starting to spin, and she twitched. Not worth it. Whatever it was. Not worth it. Emmett could fish it out. Emmett.

His keys were on the entry hall table. Maybe he went for a walk. She'd clean it all up and then have a fresh glass of wine waiting for him. He always felt better after a walk. Nearly always. She'd clean it up, but first she ran back up the stairs and grabbed the box, it was so light. Ran it straight downstairs to the front door. She paused in the doorway, looked to see if he was coming back up the street. Empty. She ran next door, put it on Denver's porch. There. When Emmett came back she could tell him, the box was already out of the house. And she'd order in, to make up for the chicken. And she'd plan, you know, meals. So this kind of thing couldn't happen again.

TERRI, TWO DAYS AGO

The shovel didn't work. Terri tried to get the point of it in between the floorboards in the living room but the hardwoods were tightly packed. Not that she wasn't happy they were hardwoods, she was happy, she was so happy. She couldn't imagine trying to do this with carpet. Carpet fibers hiding little... ugh. They'd torn the carpet up way back when she learned about the formaldehyde and other chemicals baked into the fibers. Or the fibers were made from chemicals? She couldn't remember. Didn't matter this was worse. She ran to the garage and came back with a screwdriver, lined up the flat end on the seam between two boards and tried to jam it in there. She looked around for something to pound into the handle but most of the furniture was turned over and the drawers were dumped. The stuffing from the couch cushions covered most of the floor, how was she supposed to find anything? She needed the hammer. She really needed a chainsaw, but she wasn't going to drive in this weather, whatever it was. Rain or hail or wind it couldn't make up its mind. And thinking about the weather made her think about her partner, and how he hauled JD off with him to his mother's. Please. Like she couldn't have this all back together in a jiffy so they could do movie night and where is that hammer? She sat back and wiped the sweat off her forehead. Where had she last seen it? The closet.

Terri ran upstairs two at a time which was hard to do because the tile they spent three months choosing for the facings was chipped and shattered all over the steps. It wasn't her fault. She walked in on JD's bath time and saw the tub full to the brim with those brown wriggling bodies crawling all over her baby, her little one, and maybe, maybe she screamed this time and maybe it scared JD but what was she supposed to do? They wouldn't stop coming out of the drain even though she turned it off and then JD was playing with them, playing with them like they were bubbles, and it was only when her partner pulled her from the room and put her into their bedroom, asking her, begging her, please, please stay there he would handle it, he would take care of it. Well, that was fine, but that was hours ago. And slightly less than hours ago, when he popped his head back into the bedroom, she grabbed him and asked him if they were gone he stared for a moment then said sure, yes, of course, of course all the bugs were gone, not bugs she said, they were earwigs disgusting disgusting earwigs, and he said yes all gone and he just needed her to stay in the bedroom, stay there, he was taking JD to his mom's which was fine that's fine that an excellent idea because at that very moment she saw a tiny brown body slip between the door to the closet and the frame so she nodded at her husband oh yes dear excellent, I just need a little rest, and the moment the car pulled out she was in the garage grabbing the hammer and on the way back up the stairs she saw another brown body so she smashed all the tile as she went up each step smash smash smash— three quick hits to get every bug before she went after the little monsters in the closet. At least that's how she remembered it, now that she was standing in the bedroom again, looking at the holes in the plaster, pulling the hammer out of the wall.

DENVER, TWO NIGHTS AGO

Denver had the dream again. The one that wasn't a nightmare anymore, because she'd worn the edges off. Here's the aisle of the grocery store. Here's the cart, pressed against her stomach, pushing it with her torso as much as her hands, the wheels grinding slower and slower. There's the guy, who looks at her ass as she walks by. When she turns back to her cart, Alaric is gone, climbed out again. She hears a giggle one aisle over, but she can't see him of course through the shelves, and as she shifts her eyes back to her own aisle it stretches out before her, doubled, tripled in size. She tries to run to the end but her hands are stuck, she's wearing gloves suddenly in that weird dream way, gloves that are welded to the cart and reach all the way to her shoulders, and she remembers them, from the incubator remembers even in her dream joking with Janey about how alien they look, how robotic, and then how much it killed her that that was how he'd first feel their touch but it doesn't matter because her hands won't come out here and now in this dream they are stuck won't slide or even budge so she can run free of the cart and find him. Find him. Someone find him. She suspects she's thrashing, possibly punching but she has to get her hands free. She wrenches against the cart and finally her hands pop out of the gloves and send her flying down the aisle in the wrong direction. She can't turn around, there's nothing behind her she has to get to the other end of the aisle as it slides further away so she screams but she can't scream, she can't scream even as her throat pushes air out of her mouth, she's certain that's how it's supposed to work isn't it? Isn't it? If you can just get enough air... she feels her gut pushing, abdomen clenching dry heaving.

Shit.

Her heart slams against her chest, pushing to break free of its cage and even so she knows it's a dream. Too familiar to be called a nightmare, too familiar. Familiarity didn't stop the ache in her chest as she woke in their bed, the rapid flutter focusing everything just there, just off center, pound pound pound radiating out and sucking all of her into it, empty and full. Just there.

The sheets were remarkably smooth when she finally unraveled her head enough to see them. And the warm form beside her slept on, a soft snore telling her to rest, just rest. She took a breath, unclenched her shoulders, then her hands. Lips together. Teeth apart. She remembered Janey remarking, oh so long ago, 'I can feel the tension coming off you. It's like sleeping next to a tightly wound...something.' Here the metaphor fell apart in that Janey way, that casual drift onto something else not quite sure when this painting will be done until someone has already purchased it. Same thing. Denver understood the message even without the end of the sentence. It wasn't that complicated. Unlike the paintings Janey created which were complicated. Complicated, and more often than not, sold while she still considered them incomplete. Denver asked her once, when they were still dating and had time to discuss such things – how could she part with them? How could she let them go if she didn't think they were done? Janey shrugged and pulled out a fresh canvas. "I figure it's a conversation. Who am I to say when it's supposed to start?"

"Wow," Denver had replied, "You're kind of a pretentious shit."

Janey just grinned.

Denver hadn't been surprised to learn her new girl was an artist, or a successful one, when they met at the gallery across from the restaurant where Denver waitressed. Probably would have met her later even if she hadn't gone to see the great Janey's installation. It was doors. The installation. Doorways, and doors, and windows. Some opened. Some didn't. And inevitably, closing one door opened another door in the gallery, but not right away. Later, Janey said the best part was listening to people decide what it meant. So much talk. Too much. Which was why when Janey found Denver, leaning against the wall not talking, she decided to see how long they could stand there, not talking. And when Denver finally figured out who she was, and turned to say hello, Janey said "Shh..." and took her hand.

If they hadn't met there, they would have met at the restaurant. The gallery crowd always wandered over for drinks with names like *La Corde Sensible* and desserts called *Frülingsfest*. Most of the staff at the restaurant were artists of one type or another. Artist was no surprise. She was surprised to learn Janey's art made her money. Made her enough to buy a house in what could only be described as suburbia. "A comment on the design of the homemaker, a destruction of the contemporary palate and the subjugation and explosion of desire, side by side within the cocoon of cookie cutter culture" was Janey-During-An-Interview speak for "I want my kid to grow up on a cul-de-sac with a nice yard." In the beginning, Denver preferred the Janey who meticulously cleaned her hands after working, rather than the one who left a few drops of paint in her hair. Painted a few drops of paint in her hair, just to see if she could get the interviewer to comment on it. They did. In the beginning, Denver simply preferred Janey, whatever she did. But by the time they married, she appreciated the distance, the shield, and she understood, though they never discussed it. You can't give everything to the canvas and be expected to have something left for an interview. Knew that her Janey, the real Janey, was hers, and hers alone. Until, of course, Alaric came along.

Alaric. She told herself she was sufficiently unwound, considered going back to sleep. But what if. What if she didn't check on him, and tonight was the night he needed her for... for...

"Wound as tightly as a whatever" sighed and swung her legs over the side. Not that it mattered, Denver didn't need a metaphor to know how tightly wound she was. Metaphors didn't stop her brain from insisting she step away from the warm form in their bed and step down the hall, place a hand on his back, feel him breathe. Just a dream.

She walked to the back door to let the dog out, saw the first strands of grey and pink paint the ridge through the window as she waited. Windy. A branch was already down in the yard. This was all supposed to be done with, months ago. The wind had no business being here now, it usually hassled them during Halloween— decorations flopping, little witches nearly airborne brooms or not. The wind had no business being here. And the chill. She waited while the dog peed and scampered back to the door, gave it a scratch as if she wasn't standing right there, hand on the doorknob to let him in.

"Yeah yeah," she said, as he bumped against her leg in gratitude. Or whatever it is dogs feel when people use their opposable thumbs to help them. The box was sitting near the table, mail piled on top. At least they'd have something to keep them busy, if the power company decided to turn the power off. Lord knows battery operated anything was not allowed in the box, the holier than thou receptacle of toddler treats and parental judgement. Was that something Janey said, or something Denver thought? Batteries or no, there'd be stuff to do. Stuff Alaric hadn't seen. The wind rapped at the window, just about past asking nicely. Yeah, the power was going off at some point today. Just a precaution, the electric company would say, the entire state knowing what happened the last time. Hundreds of cars melted. People inside. Janey spent a week burning canvases, including a few that were already purchased, but the owners just kept clapping, wanted them, charred frames falling apart and all. She insisted on more money. She got it. Denver shook her head even in memory. Couldn't decide, was it guilt they felt, or were they that dumb? Janey was no help of course. Chastised her and laughed at the same time. "I'm just a reflection of the society that built me, holding a mirror up to culture and all it holds dear."

Well. She supposed she shouldn't bite the hand that fed her, to borrow a metaphor from the dog. A crack snapped her eyes to the window just in time to see a piece of "that damn pepper tree" come down over in Bobbi's yard. Neither of them wanted to claim it, because claiming it meant taking care of the ruts and bumps it created on their shared property line. They considered killing it, but only in private conversations away from the play group. Janey called it "mutual avoidance" and mocked the shared delusion. She, of course, was all in favor of "chopping the fucking thing down." She of course, also pretended to be aghast about "murdering one of nature's sentinels," a phrase she used only when she bounced into a play group chat just long enough to watch the sparks fly. Killing a tree was not going to endear anyone to Terri, group leader and resident embracer of all things arboreal. Janey said it was a better was of saying tree hugger. Denver said nothing because if you have to explain the joke.

Denver sat down at the table, her eye half smushed as her face rested deep in her palm. She flipped through the mail, tossed the competing offers from cell phone service providers in the recycle bin to fight it out amongst themselves, and pulled the wooden box closer. Pretty cover, flowers, fairies, leaves, what Janey liked to call 'earth goddess vomit' when it showed up on the plastic packaging of an equally plastic toy, and 'astonishingly unremarkable' when it showed up on someone as a tattoo. Denver asked her once if she ever got tired of being the only person on the planet who knew the real deal and she just laughed and said 'that's why they pay me the big bucks, I'm the one.' Then she buried her head in Denver's neck and a few other places while Denver inquired further, because inquiring minds want to know, 'did she have an answer for everything?' Janey was sliding Denver's underwear to one side with her tongue and she looked up long enough to grin, breathe out low and warm and say, 'so far so good.' And it was.

She considered what might happen if she went back and snuggled up against Janey, there at the end of the hall when her hands flipped open the box and she nearly barfed, oh god the smell was rancid. She held her breath, took a small careful sip of air. The smell paused too, then slid out a moment later and punched her in the nose, made her eyes water. She let the lid fall shut. What the hell. Dumpster came to mind, overlaid with something burnt, maybe hair. Or plastic? Or maybe dishwasher residue, that scent that came out with the steam from the industrial dishwasher in the kitchen at work. Another joke of Janey's. "Someone has to play the starving artist" when Denver told her she was going back to waitress after Alaric was born. The money was decent and she needed the adult conversation, not with strangers who were angry about their salad dressing but the other waitresses on her shift, the lot of them knew each other so well: waitresses, cooks, bus boys. Covered for each other. They pooled their tips which wasn't always great but wasn't always awful, when you were the one who got stiffed. Gagging complete, she peeked at the contents, assuming she'd see an old PB&J, or a half a banana, some remnant of snack time from over at Brenda's. There was nothing in it.

Damnit. How could Brenda drop it off without the toys? The light over the back door flickered and came back, flickered and went out as the light in the hall came on. It buzzed for a minute as Denver wondered where the candles were, not that it mattered in the pre-dawn light. Plenty of time to figure all that out. She could just as easily go back to bed. She could hear the hum of the bulb, and had just walked over to stand underneath it when the hall flooded with light pouring out of the living room. She rounded the corner and even as her brain said fuse box it felt like too much light. She couldn't see it, you see. The living room. It was bright and golden and enormous, like the gallery, or no, the restaurant maybe? Where was she? She braced her hand on the door jamb and looked, no one she recognized. No one she knew or that knew her. Or was it that she couldn't catch their faces, why were they looking away? She stepped in and they moved around her, gracefully drifting to the sides as she walked, straight through the crowd for once, not stepping to the side, tray overheard to wait as they passed. She walked straight through. Straight through to the mirror and when she reached it, she looked back at her empty living room. The lights flickered again, pulsed bright and then retreated, the buzz held even as it dimmed to just a lamp on a table. Just a lamp. In a room. Her room. Her living room.

She looked at the mirror and caught a smudge in her reflection, rubbed it but that only made it worse. What did it matter? She sat down in the chair next to the lamp, opened the small wooden box which was not covered in fairy puke but paint, courtesy of Alaric. A first Mother's Day gift from him, and Janey insisted he did it himself, in spite of still being in his own clear box at the hospital. She remembered worrying that it looked like a plastic coffin, that he looked more than fragile, he looked like he was already gone that day Janey wheeled her over to the NICU. Two layers, then, glass and plastic lay between them. Janey said not to worry, he was fine. He is fine, he's great she said—and look—his first work. The little wooden box was splashed with color, hot pink and neon green, every brush stroke his, Janey swore. She flipped it open and shut, a tiny mouth with nothing to say but click as she thought about the mountains of art he'd created since. Janey insisted on referring to him by art phases rather than age or say, when he got his teeth.

"Remember his Pollack phase?" was the splattering of every meal on the wall. And the Calder phase was his tendency to play with cords, tangle them into balls and leave them around the house. Falling off his trike was an attempt at rearranging his face like Picasso until Denver wanted to scream so loud she bit her tongue. She sucked at the coppery taste. Glanced down at the tiny box. It held a little silver needle, and a strand of his hair she didn't remember cutting. Maybe Janey had? During that "remnants sculpture phase" the one where she insisted she could assemble and sell whatever they had on hand? No, no. Even Janey wouldn't sell him.

Not when they sat, without words, without him, in the hospital room and then in this room. One staring out the window, one at the floor, waiting for the next time they could visit him. Waiting until he finally came home with them.

Denver took the needle and carefully threaded one of his hairs into it, doubled it over and wound the ends around her fingertip. Rolled it to the end, letting it loop over itself so her thumb and middle finger could pinch and slide it into a knot. Threaded. She hesitated for just a moment, where to start, the side, or the middle? The side. No, her tongue. The bite stopped bleeding but she could feel the flap, lumpy against her cheek. It was easy, one stitch in and out. So much thread left. What next?

The side. She bit off the hair and reknotted it, careful not to pull out the stitch in her tongue.

She pushed the needle into her bottom lip at the edge, just under where it met her top lip and then reached inside to pull it through and out her mouth. The knot was outside her mouth and she considered briefly if she should start again, put it inside, make it neater, but she rubbed it and it felt round and good under the pad of her finger and a little voice in her head said it would look like a beauty mark which seemed too adorable so she left it. Pushed the needle back out through her top lip and her skin stretched further than she thought possible. It emptied of color before breaking, then the tiniest dot of blood appeared, and then the silver point of the needle filled the red dot and then some. She pushed her lip back along the length of it with the other hand, back against her teeth to expose more of the needle, grasped it and pushed it again through the soft skin of her mouth, her lower lip, the lip Janey liked to pull with her teeth when she kissed it in some weird homage to Pierce Brosnan of all people. At least that's what she said at the time. Stitching wasn't coming any faster, but Denver had time, she knew, it was early daylight still. The needle was getting slippery now, though it wasn't shiny anymore. She looped it again inside her mouth and stuck it through her top lip probably the last stitch she'd be able to do from inside her mouth, there just wasn't room left to maneuver the needle. She pressed the open side of her lips together and stitched from the outside then, and it was ragged and uneven and altogether not as neat as she would have liked, if she could have liked it, there in the chair, next to the lamp, in the living room.

Janey found her, in a shaft of sunlight that glazed the room and lied about the weather, as hailstones bounced off the glass but no matter. Janey found her, carefully tearing the stitches out for the third time, her lips a ragged ruffle, one thick line of blood drawn down her chin, down her neck, her shirt soaked in sweat and blood. Her fingertips pricked and bleeding, pushing the needle in, trying to neaten up the sides. Trying to get the pieces of flesh to line up just right. Just right. And Janey said, "Jesus Christ Den. Jesus Christ." But Jesus wasn't there, hadn't been there for a while. And anyway what did he know about sewing? Hail stones bounced and rain rolled down the roof. Little chunks of ice bashed around on the ground and the sunlight made them sparkle.

TERRI, TWO DAYS AGO

Cleaning the box started well enough. She brought it inside, put it up on the table in the kitchen. Storm clouds were rolling up at the edge of the valley, so she closed the kitchen window against the new wind. Slipped off her shoes and made a mental note to call Jean back for her new address. She'd call again, make sure she sorted it before Jean's birthday. Let the group know. That was the problem with being organized, people expected you to continue it indefinitely. They teased her, but without her they'd still be waving at each other from their driveways. At least she did something.

She had a little while before she needed to deliver the box, so she poured her third cup of coffee. Ran a damp cloth over the lid to get the layer of dust that everything in southern California had if left outdoors. The flowers on it looked nice, and she tried not to think about the thing inside. Maybe she'd ask Janey later, she might recognize it. Janey was an artist and artists knew stuff. Janey was a weirdo if she was being honest, but she definitely added a little excitement to the neighborhood. Their own local celebrity. Terri wasn't familiar with her artwork; was pretty sure it wasn't the kind of thing she'd have put on her wall in her dormitory oh so long ago. Still. A celebrity and an artist, even if she didn't fit what Terri thought of as artistic. Changed her hair color a lot. Guess that was something.

She left her mug in the base of the coffee maker for later and as she did, a little brown body squished itself under the backsplash. What the— earwig. Gross. She could see a tiny antenna sticking out and got a knife to go after it when a thud, almost like a knock on the door made her spin around. The lid of the box was rattling ever so slightly, bouncing up just enough to make a thunk when it came back down. She watched it vibrate with her back pressed against the counter, knife in hand. She dropped it when the top flew off and the earwigs began pouring out of it, rolling and tumbling, bodies catching the light. They looked like beads, or if she hadn't been disgusted, jewels, a river of gemstones flowing off the table and onto the floor. She grabbed a dishtowel, smacking at them and stomping on the ones on the floor but they kept coming, until the box wasn't a box but a mound.

For every one she squished beneath her stocking feet another five started crawling up her legs until she was dancing in place trying to throw them off and step on them as fast as she could. Still they came. Billowed out of the box, erupted with tiny scuttling legs and then she heard the clicking, clicking you could never hear with just one, but multiplied a thousand-fold clicking so loud from tiny pincers. It filled her ears and she wondered. What could they possibly want? She backed away from the box and felt one on the ridge of her ear, almost impossible to feel against the roar of the mass of writhing little bodies, she screamed with her lips pressed together so they couldn't pour down her throat. Too much. It was too much.

"Mom?"

Her eyes snapped open, already reaching for him, already protecting him from...from...

The kitchen was empty. The box sat where she left it.

BOBBI, LAST NIGHT

The wind blew the back door open, startling Bobbi from the overstuffed chair she sat in, head bobbing as she tried to read by candlelight. She caught it before it banged into the wall a second time, had to shut and open it twice more before the lock would catch. That was that problem, living in Southern California. Even when you didn't feel the earthquakes, there were always little shakers that messed up the doors, pushed the jambs just out of whack enough to make closing them a new and different experience every couple of months. The back door had been stuck for weeks, requiring an extra shove to get it closed. And now this. Swinging free of its own accord. Of course, this was a spectacular wind, the electric company already turned off the power. Had to make sure the transformers didn't blow. Couldn't lose another town to wildfires.

She wanted to talk to Denver about it, bitch about it really, when she went to pick up the toy box but Denver was gone, off with Janey to the hospital, some kind of accident. She'd seen her, walking to the car, Janey's arm around her waist, Denver's hand covering her mouth, blood dripping down her arm. Their little guy was standing on the front step when Bobbi rushed over, offered to take him so they could take care of whatever that was. No, it was no problem, no don't even worry about it, catch up later. And she held Alaric's hand, held her breath as she watched them pull out, Janey without a wave and Denver staring at her little boy, forehead pressed to the car window.

It was nothing to go inside with him, nothing to grab a little backpack, a few clothes, nothing to give him a juice box, once she figured out that's what he wanted as he struggled with the lock on the cupboard. She grabbed the toy box on the way, may as well, she'd need it with two of them to entertain. Denver had looked tired. It was an odd thing to notice on a friend whose entire shirt was covered in blood, but she remembered her eyes. They seemed worn out. Dull.

Bobbi was happy to help with Alaric, she guessed Janey was just going to drag him to the hospital with them. She looked a little panicked. And she might not have called Bobbi anyway, what with her being new. Five years after they arrived, still "new," at least according to Terri. She and Denver laughed every time she said it. Well. The Millers house was for sale so she would no longer be new. She wondered if Terri would stumble around not saying new the same way she stumbled around not saying black. That woman exhausted herself. New. Her friends from back home acted like they'd been gone forever, and so far. Moved clear across the country. Moved. Ran. Same thing sometimes. Bobbi told them it was for work and they didn't buy it, but they didn't push her. She was offline so she didn't have to see pictures of old friends. Or their kids. Still. They eventually started sending holiday cards, each family growing, faces filling the frames, a clever comment pre-printed in the corner. Requiring nothing of the sender or the receiver. Oh, she knew she was supposed to study them, the kids in particular, how each had grown, who was missing teeth, who was taller than their parent. 'Can you believe it?' scrawled on the back when a teen, a mere child moments before, became a driver. She dropped each one in the garbage bin before she even got back in the house. Kept her distance.

She peeked out the front door while she waited, palm trees genuflecting in the wind. They were made for this at least. Sure, they lost their dead leaves. Fronds. Lost their fronds, which didn't drift down so much as drop like a rock, each one as long as a car and nearly as heavy. But they had no branches to break, nothing for the wind to grab and tear. Not like that tree in the back yard that dropped a branch onto the roof of the back porch in the middle of snacks that morning, the crack loud enough to be heard over the wind and set the dogs barking. Trina sat at the breakfast table, both hands over her ears, screaming, and Alaric, Alaric didn't seem to sweat it. Bobbi had shoved the dogs into the garage and come back to the table to sooth her girl.

"Shh… it's just the tree. Hey there, how about that new box of toys?" Trina stopped yelling immediately and smiled, her tiny teeth like a jack o'lantern grin. Bobbi pulled Alaric from his chair to get a head start. Trina's head tucked perfectly under her chin as they walked to the living room. Her daughter reached down with her legs and stretched herself off of Brenda's hip to the floor, already opening the top of the toy box. Pulled out toys one by one and tossed them over her shoulder, while Alaric wrinkled his nose, and said "Poop." She hoped he didn't mean his pants, he pointed at the box and said, "Stinky poop." Maybe he didn't like the flowers on the outside. Bobbi stooped to pick up a doll, not because she cared to clean while they played but because the doll was covered in marks, and the ends of its hair looked melted, singed. She sniffed it to see if Alaric had a point, but it smelled fine, so she put it back in the box and took a closer look, nothing of hers was still in it. Maybe Terri was taking this recycled toy thing a little far, most of it looked like it had been pulled from the garbage to be honest. Maybe she was being unfair, there in her new house with the new furniture and the new curtains and the new start. It was supposed to be formal. The living room. The other moms asked if she needed a decorator when they realized there wouldn't be a moving van arriving, but she deferred. It was better to pick things out herself. It took longer. Ate up the days, sometimes the nights, shopping online drifting site to site, like finding the perfect end table mattered so fucking much it kept her up. Stuffed her brain looking for stuff.

She couldn't do that tonight though. No power. She settled back into her chair and relit the candle next to her. She had a camping lantern but candlelight was warmer, and she curled her legs up under her blanket to read. The fact that she could barely see the words in the dim light was irrelevant. She read the way she always did now, eyes moving over words that held their meaning just long enough to get her to the end of the sentence. Some even captured her, for a while. And then the inevitable ending, the final closing of the book. Plot forgotten by the time she slid it back onto the shelf. They were just stories after all. The wind came in through corners and crevices it wasn't supposed to know, and she suspected their long-distance inspection all those years ago maybe wasn't as thorough as they thought. She felt the wind push at the edge of the door as she clicked the lock, streamline itself into a whistle at the edges. At least the rain wasn't like the east coast storms of her childhood. All flash and thunder, crash and rumble and sheets of rain so thick they tripled the glass, turned it old-timey. Wavy.

Trina was out sharing her Daddy for a bit with Alaric. They were driving around looking for a fast food place that might still be open, still have power in all this wind, because her husband made the mistake of mentioning take out in front of Trina, and she held on tight and wouldn't let it go, the way kids do. He finally took both kids with him, just to go for a ride, because he knew he was the one who opened that door and their little one was dancing on Bobbi's last nerve. She watched him carry both of them to the car, one squealing kid on each hip as he pushed through the wind. He looked so balanced that way, so even and right that she turned away before the door was closed. She puttered after they left, before settling in to pretend to read. Swept because she couldn't vacuum. Wiped counters she couldn't see as the wind blew through the vents, brought god knows what into the house. Allergies she assumed. She had enough stories thanks. Enough ghosts.

She regretted it the moment she thought of it, of course. Ghosts. As if the general mention could wake them up. Call their names. Just to prove she could she walked into the dark living room, then realized who knows what was left out of the toy box. Her slipper brushed against something, and she reached down. The doll of course, missing its head now because that's what dolls do. She couldn't see, didn't know where the box was, so she walked back to the den at the back of the house and grabbed the flashlight from the table. The light spilled sharp for a moment, drowning out her candle and then faded fast to a dull orange. Even less to read by than her candle, but enough to see where she was going. The doll, or doll's body anyway, was still in her grasp and she realized she was holding hands with it, just as she had with Alaric just that morning. Her hand felt cold, achy, and she wanted to stretch her fingers, work out the pain but the doll moved. Tugged on her hand. No. No—the doll was pulled out of her hand.

Something below her pulled its leg and she and let go. It was in her hand, she was certain. How else could she have felt it when it tugged away? Even as it happened the distinction mattered. She didn't drop it, it was pulled and like it heard the argument in her head the doll didn't fall all the way to the floor, didn't move at all just hung there, upside down, one leg firmly grasped by nothing at all. Not nothing though. Something. A shadow, tight and more perfect than it should have been more perfect than it could have been. A profile, small and perfect and familiar and impossible and gone, when she tried to see it.

And then the doll moved. Moved away down the hall, bobbing slightly and then hanging still, rhythmic and slow, and she realized she'd seen that motion before, the stutter steps of new legs, gait wide and unsteady, and the lightest pat pat pat of bare feet on the tile just registered in her ear when the doll stopped moving and the footsteps stopped with it. Bobbi twisted her legs away but her eyes locked, stiff, her eyes took in the doll and the doll drifted to the floor. As if placed. As if the holder bent tiny, knobby knees and let the doll rest there, in the hall, next to a plant Bobbi knew and couldn't recall, a plant whose leaves bent ever so slightly, brushed to the side as someone passed by the alcove under the stairs. Someone she couldn't see in the pale orange light of the flashlight even as she swept it across the floor. Someone whose steps faded into less than air. It was so still. The wind waited, gathered. Waited again.

She realized she was breathing when she heard herself exhale, her head tilted to the side, arms dangling exactly where they'd been when the doll touched the floor ten feet away, standing exactly where she'd been when the plant moved there in the alcove under the stairs. The ache in her hand as she stretched her fingers, tried to bring herself back to her body. It was a draft she told herself as she calculated the likelihood of a draft moving around corners. Like it mattered. Like her body cared what her brain made of it all. Her body missed him, the smell and sound of him, the feel of his little hand patting her shoulder when she carried him. She waited for the ache to go back to its hiding place.

She turned the flashlight off to tell herself she could, to tell herself it wasn't fear, and it wasn't, because she knew he couldn't be there. He couldn't be. Could he? Told herself she was being ridiculous. Forced herself to walk back toward the living room. Forced herself to listen to her own footsteps, one by one. Forced those steps to slow, to nearly halt, to walk over to the doll and stop right next to it. Made herself count, count to ten, count to twenty like a dare. Made her body wait and bend and pick it up. She let the light from the flashlight drift away as she reached for it, fingertips touched skin somehow made soft. And when it was in her hand again she made herself hold it there, down by her side. Within reach. And then she walked. Measured, slow, some bizarre claim over every step, some insistence that she could do it, she would do it. Slowly. Counted even, between steps, made herself count there in the quiet of the house, the house the wind left altogether, preferring to stay outside, whispering at the windows but not coming in because the wind knew this story. Told this story over and over.

By the time she crossed the front hall, the cold made her fingers cramp and when her feet reached the carpet a shiver rolled through her shoulders, so she stopped. Held still. Moved the flashlight in a deliberate arc towards the box. Took a step. Made herself breathe between each foot fall, softer now on the carpet and barely audible. Softer. She reached the box and lifted the lid still holding the doll, still offering the doll, still daring someone to take the doll, when the front door slammed open at the same time the lights blazed back on and she gasped, turned her head to see her

Trina, her little one held in her daddy's arms, and another one too, a boy, her boy there on his daddy's hip, there, framed in the doorway, porch light streaming around them, paper bags and go cups in hand, and then the whole image tilted to the side and away as she fell to the ground. She felt her heart clench once and then it skipped, and she felt a tiny hand slip into her own there on the living room floor in the new house in the new town in the end.

TERRI, THREE DAYS AGO

Unbelievable. Terri dumped the bin over and a couple of blocks and a car fell on top of the toys already on the floor. She flipped it back and saw what may or may not be a snot rag sticking to the bottom, and a sticky stain that looked suspicious. Just her luck. She sighed as she sprayed it with her earth friendly spray cleaner and reminded herself that when she set up the rotation among the play group moms, she purposefully put herself at the end, so she could clean up whatever mess. Doing her best to keep it going, saving the earth one unbought toy at a time. They laughed when she suggested it between snide comments about limits and positive parenting when the latest playground scuffle broke out. Brenda in particular seemed skeptical, as she helped her daughter to the "adults only" snack tray she guarded from the other kids like a pit bull over a kitten. But then again Brenda was always skeptical of anything she didn't think of. When they say kids keep you young Terri didn't think it would turn her friends into snarky tweens again.

She realized her microfiber cloth was hot in her hand from scrubbing. No luck on the stain. Great. She set the box aside to use for... something. She didn't love that it was plastic to begin with, but she sacrificed her "no plastics" rule for durability and the chance to sanitize it between kiddos.

For the first few weeks it went well – everyone brought a toy to get it started, then rotated the box among the kids so there was always something new to play with. Even Brenda admitted that her little precious enjoyed it, and of course she bought brand new toys to put in it. Terri bit her tongue when she was tempted to remind her the point was to stop being mindless consumers and share what they had because for kids "new to them" is as good as new. At least that's what she learned growing up, hand-me-down everything. And there's nothing wrong with that.

Great. The snot rag was permanently adhered. She'd have to come up with something new to put it all in. The box appeared as if she'd asked for it, across the street at the Millers. What used to be the Millers. Divorce and unemployment doing what they will to a mortgage, which is mainly to add pressure and increase the volume of the arguments until they were impossible to ignore, windows open or not. Terri was certain someone was going to bring it up at the neighborhood meeting, but then they were gone. No idea where Mr. Miller, really Tom, really Jean's husband as she always thought of him, went. And Jean was three states away, staying with her mother. Sign of the times. Generations reunited, like it or not. Terri dialed as she looked at it. Jean picked up after three rings.

"Hey Jean, how are you? Did the moving vans finally arrive?"

"Just got here yesterday. I made the guy stand there while I counted every box."

"Yeah, that's the thing, I think they forgot one."

"Those assholes."

"It's outside on the lawn, near the, near the For Sale sign." There was a pause.

"Well then that's not mine. My stuff was in the house. That must be the shitheads, he put everything he didn't want outside and the rest of the crap in his trunk. He took his weights, but I had to ask him if he wanted a picture of the kids, can you believe that? I gotta go. My mother is trying to make lunch. Mom! MOM! Don't—"

The line cut off. Terri recalled a pile of stuff, about two weeks ago. Day by day it dwindled as passersby took this bit or that item. She didn't remember seeing the box but maybe it was hidden under the other stuff. Only the box was left, tucked beneath the For Sale sign sat just off the driveway, a couple of bored succulents making a valiant effort against the cold. It looked about the right size, she'd check it out. A jacket would have been a good idea, but instead she clutched her coffee, pressed her arms against her chest and hurried across the street. Her uniform of leggings and a long sleeve tee no match for the chill. She drew up short on crossing, because she thought she saw someone in the window. Just a flutter at the edge of her vision but of course there was no one there. The house was empty. Just another box of empty dreams. She snorted at herself, still pretending she worked for the station, still pretending she had to cap every topic with a little send off to the next segment. She needed to add another mediation session to her schedule. She stepped off the side-walk and was nearly hit by an SUV speeding by, Janey behind the wheel. Sweet Jesus. Two meditation sessions. Deep breath, look both ways.

The box. She stood a few feet away, facing it, sipped her coffee. It seemed clean enough. For something sitting in the dirt. And it was wooden, which was good, at least no plastic. She wondered if it was heavy though, she could imagine Brenda complaining. Bobbi would suggest more planks, in her yoga fixes everything eat healthy be healthy mind over matter way. It was fine, Terri preferred it to Brenda's bitching, but she wondered if it's what Bobbi really thought. She felt like Bobbi was holding back, and why wouldn't she? She was the only black woman in their group, and while Terri told herself that she, Terri, would never think about it, she did. But Terri was determined not to see color. Or to see it but not differentiate it. Or to acknowledge it but not discuss it? Or... she wasn't sure what she was determined to do, but it was mostly not to act like an asshole if at all possible. Probably too late.

The box just sat there. It had two wooden handles on either side, four in total which seemed weird and only added to her worry that it would be heavy. She stepped closer and saw a faded decoration burned into the lid. Something, something almost like a fairy, or it reminded her of a garden, maybe. Pretty. Good. One of the boys in the group needed reminding that not everything in the world had to be skulls and danger and smashing things. The first week of the rotation a puzzle came back with the pieces chewed; she'd warned them not to include puzzles but no matter. Denver tried to tell them all that it wasn't their son, that it was their dog, but Terri knew it was that little demon child. He was singlehandedly destroying the idea of that men weren't toxic from the get-go. Little asshole. And who names their kid Alaric. Someone named Denver she guessed. Fine. That determined it, fairies and flowers or whatever the hell those decorations were, she was using this box.

She marched over to it, grabbed the handles on both sides. She lifted it fast and utterly overcompensated for the weight, nearly smacking herself in the face. She put it down again, checked the edges, lifted the cover. There was another engraving on the bottom, not exactly fairies and flowers this time. Deep grooves, black and burnt formed a door. Maybe a window? That part was rendered too flat to determine. Didn't matter because something was crawling, or maybe falling, out of that window and it turned to look at her. Woah.

She walked around to the other side but couldn't get the image right side up. It was like one of those optical illusions, where you can see one of two things depending on where you focus. Only, only she couldn't see the other thing, or any one thing. It kept shifting away from her. She couldn't put it together, just saw pieces—a hand, an eye. Flashes. A tongue. That eye again. And what the fuck is that a spoon? Okay enough. She was freezing. She stepped back and squinted. The whole thing looked homemade, like it was done with one of those wood burning kits her brother had back in the day. It was the eye that was the problem. No question it was looking straight at her, and two tones of wood shouldn't be able to do that. Had to admire the artistic skill, there, even if it did give her a shiver that nearly spilled her coffee. Well. She'd cover that up with some fabric or something and see what the world wide interweb had to say about covering demons of hell.

Terri looked both ways and walked the box back over to her house. It was the right size, it was light, it was sturdy. A thorough cleaning with a non-earth threatening cleanser ought to do the trick. Maybe she'd give the toys a once over as well. Given that state of that snot rag she'd found. As Terri carried the box into her house, she saw an ear wig, brown and wriggling, near the front door. She smeared its body across the step with the scrape of her gym shoe.

TERRI, RIGHT NOW

Three hours past sunrise. She waited. She wasn't going to waste the box; damnit it was a perfectly good box. Every now and then she stood up, walked to where she could see behind it, just in case. Just in case something came out the back. The sun shifted the shadows and light around and she curled in on herself, absently picked at the skin flaking off her forearms. A car pulled up in front of her driveway. An officer stepped out.

"Morning."

"Morning," she said, eyes still on the box.

"Do you have a moment? We'd like to talk to you about your neighbor, Mr. Miller."

She turned her eyes away from the box to meet his stare.

"When was the last time you saw him?"

<hr>

THE DEEP END OF THE POOL

<hr>

"little children it is the last hour"
(John 2:18)

THE CHILD LAY ON HER BELLY WATCHING THE HEAT WAVES rise off the sidewalk. It should have burned her stomach, but the warmth felt good, so she flipped onto her back to stare into the sun. The woman caught her, yelled about her eyes again, about her dress crumpled up beside her again. She moved slowly as they hollered at her to get in the car already. Even so, she was in back waiting as they tossed towels in the trunk, the woman balancing two containers and a lit cigarette while she cranked the windows down. They fiddled with chairs, worried over pasta salad congealed in the heat. She slid over the vinyl seat to the shady part. The man and the woman were sweating in the glare, damp and sticky and irritable. The child tucked her feet up on the seat. It was cooler and she couldn't smell the cigarette as badly from the shady side. She watched the ash grow longer and longer and finally scatter on the driveway as they backed up.

You glance over the back of the seat and she's staring at you, eyes tight on yours. What is wrong with this child? She was lying on the sidewalk, again, just staring at the sun when you came out of the house. Her dress crumpled in the dirt, flip flops on the wrong feet. Still a little girl, so there was time to fix whatever this was. Off. She was off somehow. She should have been cute at this age, maybe even pretty, but her eyes were too old for her face. An old soul your mother said, but what did your mother know, you found her naked in the garden again and the doctor just shrugged. You look away from the old soul's eyes, but you can still feel them on you. At least she didn't complain when you pulled a brush through her hair, tugged it into a ponytail while she stood there, staring. She never cries, at least there's that, no matter how hard you yank the brush. And you yanked it hard. Told yourself you were working on a knot. Well. You tried. She looked the part: little bathing suit and sunglasses she refused to wear. Staring into the sun – what kind of child does that for that long, without even blinking? Stubborn. Even as a baby she never cried. Refused to snuggle while she nursed, but oh how she made you bleed. You wince, recall desperately shoving a finger between her mouth and your breast, her gums crushing it, crushing your tender skin even as it tore open. Your husband laughed when you told him, brushed it off. Nipples can't bleed he said, not from a baby, even as the blood smeared your chest and she vomited it back at you, black and thick. He didn't bother to look. But that was long in the past and thank god for formula. Today was about friends. Friends, and maybe a chance to forget for a little while.

"Won't it be fun, darling, to play in the pool?" the woman chirped from the front seat. And then, "Try to smile honey, have fun with the other kids." Her mother. She considered the woman everyone called her mother. Hair crispy with something that was supposed to make it curl, the frizz smoothed over with hair spray, pulled up off her neck to show a patch of pale flesh damp in the heat. Hand dangling a new cigarette. Not bothering to wait for a reply as she fiddled with the cassette tape, twisting it round and round, a long red nail stuck in the hole. So proud of that player in the car, talked about it all the time. Same song, over and over. Something about holding and folding. It didn't make any sense to the child, but it didn't have to. She watched them the way a lion watched a lizard. It required no effort but passed the time.

You see them pull up but take no notice, you're waiting for the burgers to finally finish. Pull yourself away from the downwind side of the grill, yes, there – in the driveway. The adults bolt out of the car first, balancing offerings and heading straight through the crowd to the liquor. The child is slower, she slides from the back, taking a long breath. See the shadows slide away under her feet? It's so hot. The sun is directly overheard after all, and everyone is blurry. Maybe it's the booze. There are so many children around, it's understandable. No one notices another tow head in a red and blue striped bikini, her round belly sticking out and soft limbs marked by knobs of knees and pointed elbows. Young. Four years old. Maybe. And if so, just barely. The age where stillness comes only in slumber, yet she barely moved. It may have struck you as odd when she watched for a moment, and then found a cool spot to sit in the shade, fingers raking the grass, combing the blades over and over until her nails were green and smelled like springtime. The birds waited for permission to speak again. But no matter, your burger is ready and hopefully, hopefully, not overdone.

She rested under the tree, palms pressed to the earth, and let the leaves whisper. Back against the bark, legs stretched in front, the ground filled the hollow spaces. She knew what parties were, she'd been dragged to enough. A pool party. A huge backyard BBQ, something to do with the adults. She left her sundress in the car and wandered, away from the man and the woman. They were already changing— his eyes rimmed in red, holding a sweaty glass near empty. The woman left a tinfoil covered something at a table, a fresh cigarette waving around her head trying to ignite her hair. Hot. Not hot enough to swim with your clothes on, but that's what the adults were doing.

The child moved toward the diving board and had to walk wide around a group of adults, men with soft bellies and skin unfamiliar with the sun, strange patterns of hair on their chests. Women, stripped of dignity, cover-ups covering what they could. Her nose sniffed. The stench of flesh as it burned in the sunshine, a crisp tang in the air as the cells popped under the surface of the skin. She smelled the push of new cells from underneath, determined to arrive. Sometimes the flavors were too much, and she closed her eyes. They were all overheated, turning shades of brown, of pink. Skin crisp and tight, the blood draining from the surface, leaving it to bake. Slick with sweat, it burned faster in the sun. She listened to their skin crackle and she giggled. Death didn't offend her.

"Hello little lady," his mouth boomed from atop a mountain of a body. She looked up, way, way up to a face marked by dripping red lips and a wisp of hair haloing his head. His belly rounded, his waist a full circumference of the globe. Nothing on but swim trunks, a sweaty glass of gin and lime in his hand. A smile.

She said nothing. He was not particularly interesting beyond the giant size of his belly, already noted. She could hear his heart straining to pull the blood from his toes, the meat of it grinding against his rib cage. A stranger. The man and the woman were somewhere else, near the screaming, screeching women being tossed in the pool. Adults and alcohol really don't mix. She moved to pass around him when her feet left the ground and her body rose in the air, flung over his shoulder. Her bare stomach hit the rounded mound of skin over muscle over bone, sticky with sweat. A quick tug, and his hand pulled her bathing suit down to the back of her knees. The smack of his palm against her bare bottom. One swallow of his drink and she was back on the ground, suit pulled up, her thumb still hitched in the waist band. That fast.

She stared.

The crowd laughed. Mustaches and melting ice cubes gaping. What was he? This mountain of flesh who took her, took her from the ground. She felt heat in her face as she gazed up at him but there were no tears. Just a fingertip of white-hot anger sliding down her spine. The laughs faded, or her ears stopped working, filled with a buzz. He stared back, unknowing. Unaware.

A scream ripped the air, followed by a splash. Another jump-suited woman landed in the pool, attached to a howling face and a hand desperate to keep that drink aloft, keep that hair dry. The child held the eyes of the man until he glanced away, had to look away, oblivious to the injury taking root.

The first tiny tear of muscle from muscle, the first quiver in his overworked heart as the cells shredded and died, leaking as they tore. It wouldn't take long, the organ nearly exhausted itself with each heartbeat. She stood her ground until he rubbed his chest, held the moist glass to his skin to cool the burning sensation deep inside.

The child moved on and found the diving board, patiently waited in line as the other children moved ahead. A blond boy, hair buzzed short. A girl, bathing suit hitched up too high, a stripe of pale skin next to browner skin showing at the top of her thigh as she jumped, screamed, splashed. Then the boy, hollering as he went, "Mommy! Mom! Mom! Look, look at me, look at me, look look lookit loookit lookit I'm—." His head bobbed back up gagging and spitting, "Did you see? Did you see me?"

Now. She stepped onto the board and felt the stubble, the rough surface gripping her feet as she walked straight into the water and sank to the shadow below. The heat left her face. Her gaze became cool and quiet again. She looked to the surface, waving lines and colors, cackling voices muted. One minute. Two minutes. Another body entered the water without grace, a shoulder, then a back, then an arm and a wine glass. The wine floated in the water around her for a moment, a red cloud drifting clear. Chlorine burned her nose but no matter. It was time.

You see a little girl jump into the pool and idly wait for her head to bob up again. The next child jumps, splashes, swims to the side and you think, she should be up, she should be up by now, where is she? You know it's been too long but it's impossible, isn't it? You can't be the only person to notice, where is she? Why isn't she coming up? Should you tell some-

one? Panic flutters in your stomach— you should tell someone. Tell someone. Do it. Do it now. You stand up to shout
when the ground throws you in the air and your neck snaps
against your lawn chair.

Deep below her she felt the ground shrug as she sat, a slim
plastic liner all that separated her from the earth beneath the
pool. Her fingers pressed against the plastic, nails stretching
it down into the earth until it tore. Eyes closed, head to the
side, dreaming. Her hands shoved the liner aside and pushed
into the wet dirt, water rushing into the gaps around her
arms. The shrug in the ground became a twitch, rock
slammed against rock. She released her grip.

You don't notice at first, you never do. Just a gentle sway, an
added ripple to your already wavy walk toward jello ambrosia
and wilting salad. A jostle into another sweaty body, so sorry,
excuse me, no after you and the inevitable pinch on the ass.
An open mouth laugh, oh you devil, interrupted by the slam
of your fingers between the chair and the table. You grab each
other, steady yourselves by the table but he is torn away,
mouth still open as he falls to the ground, hot dogs and
watermelon raining around him, ridiculous, a slice of his forehead hanging into his eyes. It's absurd, you think, how funny
he looks, such a startled expression, he seems confused by his
own bloody flesh and you feel a laugh lifting into your throat
but you can't keep eye contact because the table you clutch
moves with you, jumps out of reach as your knee slams into
the ground, the cap of bone popping out crushed against the
pavers, the pain radiates to your clenching stomach but you

try standing keep looking for the sound, where is the sound, where is the screamer, and you realize it's you, of course it's you, jaw locked open as your eyes search and search for a safe place, a sanctuary.

There. A tree.

Straight and tall and strong, you turn to it as a wave rolls through the lawn, as you tumble backwards to the edge of the pool, your hand somehow still holding your glass. It's funny, that's funny, you want it to be funny but your mouth is filled with blood and broken teeth, you choke and spit and see his forehead again, flapping, the bone beneath it wet. You try to sink your body into the earth, try to attach it somehow to slow things down, to make it all— please, please slow down please stop please stop... you are above the ground, it pulls away from your hip, your shoulder, before slamming back into you. As your blood stains the cement, it buckles, makes impossible curves and bumps until it splits open against your skull. You hang on the edge of the world, images still streaming into your brain. A little girl, sinking into the mud. You reach for her, if you can just reach her. Her lips are moving but you can't hear her over the screaming and the rushing water. The screams remind you of something you love, high pitches playing over voices low and begging, it's a rhythm, it's—oh it's music you love music it's so beautiful so beautiful you're crying. And then you hear it. Softly. So close. The thunk of your skull once. Twice. Three times against the concrete before it finally goes soft and drips over the edge of the pool, your fingers still clutching your crushed glass.

Bodies crashed into the pool, mouths open sucking in bleach and chlorine, water and piss, as the wine spurts out of their glasses. The water climbed out one side of the pool and the bodies shattered against the other, wine and blood. Water into wine, wine into blood. The ground stretched and slammed ripping itself to pieces in an effort to get to the child until finally, finally the plastic gave way as she sank, dissolved into the mud. The earth came back to itself, began to spin again. The shadows returned, grew longer, stretched over bodies and blood stains.

"She's alive!"

Floating, cradled in warm wet earth. She could feel the cracked foundation of the pool and every line where the earth seeped in to greet her. She lay on her back, eyes open, drifting. The game she'd seen kids playing in the bleached water. It took a long time for the others to arrive and find them. All of that afternoon, and now finally, deep in the night, voices came again, disturbing her as she lay resting. She didn't need the rest, but she enjoyed it. Earthquake was the word they used. It bounced around the street. There were people and microphones and lights. So many lights. She could barely see beyond them. Luckily she rarely used her eyes. The child was taller when they pulled her out than when she went in, nothing anyone would have noticed except a mom if she'd still had one. These men were gentle, but the mud was thick and soothing, and she let it keep her cocooned a while longer.

"Okay, Okay, now. Gently, gently!"

She felt hands straining to reach her, shadows crossing her lids against a blazing backdrop of electrical lights. The hum pushed into the base of her neck and irritated her. But no matter. The voice, the voice was moss and deep, deep soil. It slipped into her ears and soothed her tongue.

"It's going to be all right, little one, shh..." he said, the smell rolling off him slaked the thirst in her throat as she inhaled it deep into her pores. She knew everything was all right. She wasn't even tired; she just couldn't be bothered to move on her own when they were so willing to do it for her. And why should she? He thought the mud was the problem; it dried on her skin and hardened, encasing her, and he gently brushed it with his fingertips until the dirt rimmed his fingernails a deep black. She liked the way it looked against his skin, like layered soil, fingernail-dirt-skin, deep shades of earth and loam and rock. Past the green smells were lilacs, a woman. He lived with an older woman, the lilacs covered a chemical, a medicine, and it stung her nose. He turned to wet a cloth and the metal and oil of the gun at his hip came at her. Sharp. He'd fired it, a long, long time ago. It was too much to take in, so the child closed her eyes for a moment and breathed through her mouth until the tree brought her back, whispering, always whispering.

"All right, little one. Can you sit up?"

It was a foolish question but kind.

"Oh, what a pretty girl you are, I see you, I see you there." He brushed the last bits of dirt from her face. "It's gonna be okay, I promise. Does anything hurt?" She heard a siren, and he popped his head up, but it wasn't for them. Too many tragedies right now.

"We're just going to sit here until, until we can get you a doctor. Just a little while longer." He seemed tired, and not just from tonight. Exhaustion came in a wave from him, and she heard his breath straining. "How about... how about a smile? Can you smile?" She considered it for a moment, then looked at him tenderly, his deep brown eyes meeting hers, almost black now.

A smile slid from deep inside her, dragging its feet. It crawled higher, pressing on her tongue with the taste of bile, polishing her teeth with sick.

He looked startled, and then the sirens turned onto the street.

She forced her lips into a hard line until they darkened, nearly black. It was time. After all, they asked for her. Demanded her. She slowly eased her lips open, parted to let the smile out. It tugged at the corners of her mouth, forced its way, yanked them open, pulled and stretched until she was certain she'd tear, until she was certain she'd been split open and she gasped once, so painful, so exquisitely painful. She pushed herself deep inside to give it room, to let it breathe, and a moan escaped. Well then.

A smile slid from deep inside her, dragging its feet.

<hr>

You hear nothing. The sounds are gone, maybe there's nothing left to hear. It should be peaceful but your body is still here, still... somewhere. You sense it near you, bleeding, attached by strands and sinew, your skin a bag. Your eyes work, or your eye. It rolls in what's left of your skull and you see her, there, across the yard. The child. She's covered in mud. Alive. Someone is helping her, someone is holding her in his arms and rocking her, gently. She curls against him and looks straight at you. She's smiling, and you slip into the deep end of the pool.

DEAR READER

Dear Reader,

Thank you for reading Next Door.

The girl from The Deep End of the Pool *will return in her own full-length novel. Additional stories from the same time period as* Moo *are being transcribed as they are discovered and will be published en masse once the author determines the fate of humanity. Follow kdbwrites for the latest on Twitter, Instagram, Facebook, etc.*

Having come this far, please share your thoughts in a review - even a word to let me know what you thought is greatly appreciated. My books are open to public reviews on Amazon and GoodReads.

Have a clot free day -

KDB

IN GRATITUDE

Common wisdom states that writers work alone but I've had such excellent company on the path to this collection. First, to my patrons who made this book possible- your support cannot be overstated. Many of these stories owe their inspiration to submissions calls and online prompt shares. Many are the children of ideas that came to me as I wandered social media. Sometimes it can be a cesspool, but I find it closer to a swimming hole. Sure, there's the odd bit of muck or an occasional dead body, but I've found supportive, creative people and I'm grateful. I've never been one of the cool kids, but I waved at Gabino and Ted, they waved back and my writing life got all the weirder, for which I am grateful. Someday I will make you lasagna which will not be as good as my mom's so we'll give it up and get donuts.

To my editor Erin and cover artist Lynn – your work makes my work work and I am grateful. What great luck to find you and what a great pleasure to work with you both; I hope we can do it again soon. Grazii to Brad, my writing buddy these many years, Sarah for reminding me to move my body not just my brain, and Lluvia, who helps me in every way a friend can be a friend. Bless you all from my heart. To Beau, for your constant support of all the dark stuff and the last minute catch (in equal parts). To the bookworms I laugh with every day on IG, thank you, you strange and wonderful people. You know who you are you weirdos.

Thank you to my family, who always made me feel like I had something to say. And last but always first, the three people I love beyond reason: IDB and JSB nothing I write here could do you justice, and Danieli, mille grazii per tutti, t'amo, t'amo, t'amo. Sempre così.

Kimberly Davis Basso is an author, playwright, director, and teacher. Her first public foray into writing was a staged reading of a ten minute play back in 1996. She has two published works of non-fiction humor in addition to this collection: *I'm a Little Brain Dead* and *Birth and Other Surprises*, both of which have won prizes for humor. Kimberly is a stroke survivor, and is available as a speaker for conferences, class rooms, and book clubs.

facebook.com/kdbwrites
twitter.com/kdbwrites
instagram.com/kdbwrites

ALSO BY KIMBERLY DAVIS BASSO

I'm a Little Brain Dead

Birth and Other Surprises

Please see KimberlyDavisBasso.com

for a list of available theater scripts.